# Leaving Ah-wah-nee

## A Novel

Harlan Hague

Graycatbird Books



ISBN-9781719940054





Cover image by Christine Loberg. Donna Yee designed the cover.

# Chapter 1

Day after day, day after day,
We stuck, nor breath nor motion;
As idle as a painted ship
Upon a painted ocean.

Jason looked up at the sails, squinting in the fierce glare. The canvas sheets hung limp. Not a whisper of a breeze. He stood at the rail near the bow, alone on the deck. The other passengers were below, seeking relief from the blistering sun. Crewmen also were below, sitting on a passageway floor, leaning against a wall, or lying in bunks. They could do nothing on deck to alter the ship's condition. Nor did they wish to be on deck, not in this heat.

The sea, sparkling silver, showed not a ripple or hint of a swell. As far as the eye could see in every direction, the gray horizon blended with the pewter sky.

Pulling a kerchief from a pocket, Jason wiped his face. Why should he remember these lines at this moment? He hadn't thought about the poem for years, not since his daddy read it to him, when, fifteen years ago? He read it more than once. It was a favorite of his.

His daddy, Seth, was not schooled, at least not beyond the third grade. It wasn't too many years after Seth finished the third grade that his own father decided that it was time for the twelve-year-old to take up an apprenticeship in a blacksmith shop, only a short walk from the family farm. His father had said that it was for his benefit, to teach him to be self-reliant and proud of his capacity for work. Seth later realized that he had been put to work mainly to contribute to the family income. He had been too young at the time to protest. Later he bitterly resented that his schooling had been cut short.

Seth was a bright child, and a bright young man. Deprived of a classroom education, he read everything he could get his hands on. Since the farm was only a couple of hours on horseback from Paducah in western Kentucky, he was able to borrow books at the small library and hurry home or back to the smithy. The selection at the library was limited, but he found histories, biographies of famous people, and stories that instructed young people how to live their lives.

On arriving home, Seth would find a corner and read. After a break for chores, he returned to his book. His mother often chided him for reading by firelight. You're going to ruin your eyes, she had said, but she didn't forbid him. Seth learned later that she had not agreed with his father's decision to end his schooling.

Jason benefited from his father's experience. He attended the local school for all of the six grades available and, following his father's example, read every book he could find. Seth also read to him. These readings always had a point. At least, his father drew a lesson from each reading. You must try to understand the human condition, he often said. Try to understand why people do what they do.

As much as he enjoyed his books, Jason also loved to be outdoors. He welcomed all seasons, wildflowers in spring, the tall corn and acres of growing row crops in summer, the glorious autumn colors. He even relished the sharp cold of a winter storm.

He wondered now whether the reality of his childhood was as unblemished as the memory.

Leaning over the rail, Jason looked down at the sea, the glassy sea sparkling in the bright sunshine. He looked toward the horizon, the join of the gray sea and gray sky almost indistinguishable. He blinked and rubbed his eyes with both hands, looked again at the horizon.

> Water, water, everywhere,
> And all the boards did shrink;
> Water, water, everywhere,
> Nor any drop to drink.

He recalled that it was a long poem. He didn't recall how it ended. Maybe he didn't want to know the ending.

Now he remembered. When his father read this long poem—*what was the title?*—he said that it illustrated desperation. People who act out of desperation do not act rationally, he said. They do foolish things.

That's why I remembered this poem. No, I won't do anything desperate. That would be the coward's way. Yet . . .

He felt the slightest coolness on his cheek and looked up. The sails above his head moved, almost imperceptibly, then they were still again.

He stared at the horizon. He had been warned the Caribbean often was stormy, cold at any season, and ships had been blown off course, even capsizing and going down in heavy seas, all passengers and crew lost.

Not today. It was the hottest day since the beginning of the voyage, a journey that began in another life. The surface of the sea was a mirror, and the horizon a flat black line. He looked down at the still water at the ship's side. An object of any weight falling into the sea would cause movement, sending circular ripples slowly outward to diminish and disappear. A body falling into the sea would do that.

He shuddered. Rubbing his face with both hands, he wiped his eyes with a sleeve. He looked up at the empty sky. Had it been only a month since his life ended? It seemed a lifetime.

Three of Jason's neighbors in the late '40s had talked so much about Oregon that he was intrigued, then interested, then convinced that Oregon was their future. The word was that this far western country was replete with rich farmlands that had never seen a plow. And these vast acres were empty and available.

Never mind that the lands were occupied by Native Americans whose ancestors had lived there since the beginning of time. They were part of the wild land that would be bested by enterprising American pioneers.

Jason persuaded Jessie that they should take the leap and begin all over again in the new American province. She was easily convinced. Both their families had been moving westward for generations, always at the far edge of the frontier. Moving westward in search of something better was in their blood. They had thought their migration finished when they cleared the woodland in western Kentucky a decade ago and built their farm. The venture was successful, and it was a good farm, but now it wouldn't do.

Now they talked about Oregon incessantly, painting a picture of a paradise, a place where all their dreams would finally be realized. It would be the end of their migration.

The children, wide-eyed, became exited at the prospect of a journey over the plains in a wagon. Ten-year-old Christian and eight-year-old Nicole thought this sounded like a great adventure. The family talked about it evenings before the fireplace, the parents in their chairs, the children on the floor at their feet, looking into the embers, sharing a dream that had no rough edges.

It was mid-winter when they made the decision to go to Oregon, so they didn't get the price for the farm they might have received if they had sold in spring or summer. But once the decision to go was made, they could think of nothing but what they must do to make it happen.

Jason was not unhappy with the sale. He had calculated closely what they would need to buy the outfit for crossing the plains, with sufficient funds left over to set them up on a claim in Oregon, and the sale price of the farm was sufficient.

He bought a heavy, canvas-topped farm wagon and five stout oxen, four for the team and an extra in case one of the team went lame. Friends thought Jason extravagant for buying the fifth ox, but he ignored them. There would be no opportunities to replace a lame ox on the plains.

He had no experience with oxen. Like most of his neighbors, he had always used mules on the farm. But all the stories he heard about crossing the plains included the admonition to use oxen, which were more reliable and required less care than mules. Jason told the seller about his ignorance of oxen. That's no problem, he said. I'll teach you. The seller's farm was but five miles from Jason's, so he rode over for instruction as often as work and weather permitted.

The ox farmer taught Jason more than how to drive the docile beasts. He told Jason that he should carry a pistol on his journey. Jason had recoiled at the suggestion. I'll need a rifle and shotgun, and I have those, he had said, but pistols are only used to shoot people. The farmer replied that the pistol would protect his family. Besides, he said, maybe the mere display of the pistol could prevent violence. Jason was persuaded and practiced with the farmer's Colt Dragoon. When the instruction was finished, the farmer complimented Jason on his proficiency. You're a natural, he said.

Each time Jason returned from the ox farmer's place, or from Paducah with a load of supplies, Jessie and the children crowded around him, wide-eyed, smiling and asking questions, eager to learn more about the preparations for the great adventure that lay just weeks ahead.

Jessie talked at length about the Oregon plan with Mildred, the children's teacher at the one-room schoolhouse. The local school was in the crossroads settlement a couple of miles from the farm. It was not a town, even a village. It didn't even have a name. Everyone just called it "the crossroads." The only buildings other than the schoolhouse were a tiny church that held services about once monthly, whenever the itinerant preacher came, and a feed store. A saloon-café went broke last year and now stood empty.

Jessie was determined that Nicole's and Christian's learning would continue until they could find a school in Oregon. Mildred apologized that she did not have any materials to give her. I understand, said Jessie. She explained that she simply wanted to find ways to keep the children thinking about something other than wagons and oxen and plains and sunsets. These things will be new and wonderful to the children, she said, but she wanted them also to think about numbers and words and sentences.

The momentous day finally arrived. The family had talked about this day for weeks, this setting-out day, and everyone knew what to do. Jessie and Jason had prepared and revised lists again and again, describing the essentials they would need and could carry in the limited capacity of the wagon.

Following advice from a number of people who seemed to know what they were talking about, Jason had treated the cotton wagon covers with linseed oil to shed rain. He packed a box of tools, water containers, an axe and a spare axe. The general store clerk in Paducah estimated that he bought near a thousand pounds of food, now packed in the wagon. Bedding laid out on boxes just behind the wagon seat would be a soft space for the children.

The light snowfall this past week left but a dusting on the packed few inches, and Jason expected no problems on the road or in camps. They would arrive in Independence in plenty of time to join the encampment of other families, poised to begin the trek. When the weather broke at Independence, they would be underway.

Now all was ready. The wagon was loaded the previous day and stored in the locked barn. Jessie stood on the front porch with the couple that bought the farm. They were young, newcomers to the region, as anxious to begin a new life here as Jason and Jessie were to begin the trek to their new life.

Two neighbor couples and their children also stood on the porch. Nicole and Christian talked excitedly with their friends. Their mothers and Jessie spoke softly, wiping tears with handkerchiefs and sleeves. The new owner of the farm listened, not wishing to interfere. She laid a hand on Jessie's shoulder. The three husbands stepped away, leaned against porch posts, smoking, talking softly, chuckling.

At the sound of creaking hinges, all on the porch looked toward the barn. Jason pushed the doors from inside and tied them open. He unhooked and opened the corral gate, took the leads of the three oxen and led them out. While the porch-standers watched, he yoked two oxen to the wagon and tied the third by a lead at the back. Climbing aboard, he drove the wagon to the house, wrapped the lines around the brake handle and jumped down.

"All aboard for Oregon!" Jason shouted. The children ran to the wagon, laughing and waving goodbyes to their friends. Jason waved to the porch while Jessie said tearful goodbyes to the three women. She collected her skirts and, head lowered, eyes misty, walked to the wagon. She smiled thinly at Jason, choked back a sob. Jason took her hand and helped her up to the wagon seat.

Walking to the back of the wagon, he stopped before the smiling, waiting children. They had learned the prescribed routine well. He boosted them up and inside, tugged the short rope that held the spare ox to test the tie. He went to the front, climbed up to the wagon seat, waved again to the throng on the porch.

He looked around at this place he had called home for a decade, the barn and corral, the huge black oak that shaded most of the house, the plowed fields beyond that were no longer his concern.

"Giddyup!" he said.

The oxen leaned into the yokes, and they were gone.

The eleven-day drive from the farm to St. Louis was a test. It took some getting used to the twenty-four hour cold, occasional light snow flurries, gathering wood and building fires. Preparing meals without bread-board and sink, sitting on a log and eating, trying to stay warm before climbing into bedrolls beside the fire. Rolling out of bed during the night to throw wood on the fire.

More than once, sitting before the fire or shivering on the wagon seat, Jessie looked at Jason with a face that he knew said: Why are we doing this? He dared not ask her what she was thinking. He didn't want to share doubts that had begun taking shape from the moment he pulled away from the house.

Jason did not ignore the hardships Jessie and the children were enduring, but he tried hard to raise their spirits. He talked incessantly about what lay ahead, what they must look forward to. Spring is coming, he said, and we will soon be driving in warm sunshine through green grass and fields of wildflowers.

They were all relieved to roll into St. Louis. Jason had made advance arrangements for transportation by steamboat from St. Louis to Independence. He had pondered continuing by wagon to that jumping-off town for prairie travel, but everyone he talked with who knew anything about the journey said that he should book the steamer.

They arrived in St. Louis two days before their booking, on purpose. Jason set up camp just outside town in a gathering of expectant overlanders awaiting their own departures. He walked into the town center to visit a shop that had been recommended to him.

The proprietor beamed as Jason described the guns and accouterments he had been told he needed for the overland journey. The latest caplock Hawken rifle did not come cheap, but he decided he could afford the best. For a pistol, he bought a Colt Dragoon that looked exactly like the one he had used in practice with the ox farmer back home.

He expected to use the Hawken for meat for the pot. He would love to shoot a buffalo! He assumed he would have most use for the third firearm he bought, the double barrel Greener shotgun, for small game. He hoped he would never have occasion to use the pistol. With the clerk's guidance, he added a supply of shot, balls, several pounds of black powder and a few hundred caps. As planned from the outset, he traded in his old Leman rifle and the cheap general store double barrel shotgun that misfired more than it shot.

Jason left the shop, satisfied that the preparation for the overland journey was finally complete. Hefting the heavy hardware, he felt more secure than he had felt yesterday. He also felt a little foolish.

On the scheduled departure day, the family, holding their breaths, watched their wagon hoisted to the top deck of the steamboat along with other wagons of all sorts, all loaded with goods for the Santa Fe trade or with household goods for the trek to Oregon. The animals and assorted goods were housed on the deck below. Jessie and the children found their cabin while Jason made himself as comfortable as possible in the wagon. He would not risk theft at the verge of the real beginning of their trip.

The ship's bell tolled three times, and the vessel eased from the wharf into the current of the wide Mississippi River. After cruising but a few miles, the boat turned into the mouth of the Missouri River.

The week's journey was a respite from the toil and cold of the wagon journey from the farm. It was pleasant, though hardly uneventful, as the boat dodged floating tree trunks and submerged snags and often went hard aground on sand bars. But Jason and Jessie were spectators and were content to watch the crewmen deal with the problems. The children thought the voyage great fun. All enjoyed meals prepared by someone else.

Jason befriended another Oregon-bound traveler whose wagon was tied adjacent to his own. Each agreed to watch both wagons while the other enjoyed time with his family below. Jason and Jessie spent a most satisfying afternoon alone in their cabin while the children played with new friends in the dining room.

At the Independence landing, the family said their goodbyes to some kindred spirits they had met on board whom they were not likely to see again. Most of the new acquaintances, however, they would see again, and often, since most on board were destined to be in the same wagon train bound for Oregon.

The family anxiously watched the unloading from the upper levels of the steamer. Once everything they owned was on the wharf, Jason inspected the animals and wagon. He was relieved that the oxen had borne the voyage in good form, and the wagon and its cargo were intact. He yoked the oxen, tied the spare ox at the back, and the family climbed aboard.

It was a short drive to the meadow on the outskirts of the town where Oregon-bound wagons were gathered. Oxen and mules were hobbled or tied to wagons or posts. The ground was clear of snow, muddy with shallow pools of water in low places. Smoke from campfires swirled in the light breeze. The welcoming odor of grilling meat mixed with the pungent smell of wet manure.

Jason started to pull up on the outskirts of the encampment near a copse of red cedar and buckeye, but decided to continue into the heart of the gathering until he found an open spot. Eyeing an empty space between two wagons, he drove the team off the track and stopped. He looked at Jessie. Her attempt at a smile became a frown.

"Okay?" he said.

"Yeah, I'm okay. Hungry." They had missed lunch that day during the docking and unloading.

Nicole and Christian scrambled from the back of the wagon.

"Is this the place?" said Christian.

"This is the place," said Jason. "Last camp before we head out. It'll be a few days yet. We're waiting for sunshine and green grass. Now see if you can find some firewood." The children ran toward a stand of scrub oak at the edge of the campground.

Jason climbed down, walked around the wagon and helped Jessie down. "I'll get a fire going." He walked to an old fire circle left by a previous camper, bent and arranged stones in a circle around a layer of ashes. He straightened, flexed his back. "I'm going to talk to a bunch of people first thing tomorrow and try to get a sense of when we'll be leaving. I want to book a room at a hotel as close to the departure date as possible. It'll be nice to have a warm bath and sleep in a soft bed, the last till we set up in Oregon."

She smiled, then reached for him, desperately, held him and pressed her head to his chest. She spoke softly, muffled, into the folds of his shirt. "Did we do right? We weren't unhappy. We had a good farm. The children liked their school and their teacher. We had good neighbors, good friends. Did we do right?"

He put a hand under her chin, raised it. He kissed her lips softly, kissed her moist eyes. "It's okay to doubt. I'm told that everybody who makes this trek has doubts just before setting out, and on most days during the crossing. Just know, sweetheart, that when we reach Oregon and get our new place set up, the doubts will end. We, and a bunch of other folks, are going to open up a new country. It's going to be grand, and we're going to be in at the beginning."

She tried without success to smile, looked aside at Nicole and Christian coming, chattering and laughing, their arms full of short, dry sticks.

Two days later, Jason left the camp at first light and walked into town. He had talked on a number of occasions with locals and teamsters who knew more about Independence than he about hotels. There was only one you'll want to stay in, they told him. The National. So he walked to the National this morning and went into the lobby.

"Got a room for tomorrow night?" Jason said to the clerk.

"Yep," said the clerk. "Been pretty busy here. I take it the wagons are leaving?"

"That's so. Got a room for me?"

"I do. Last one. You're lucky. We were full till one hour ago. Fella came in and canceled. Said he and the missus agreed they were on a fool's errand, and they were going home."

"I hate to benefit from someone's misfortune, but I'll take it on this occasion."

The clerk nodded, pushed the register to Jason. "Sign here, please. I'll need payment in advance." He smiled. "Since you'll be off early."

"I understand. And you're right." Jason signed the register. He pulled a small leather drawstring pouch from his pocket and counted out some quarter eagle gold coins.

At that moment, the front door burst open. A disheveled character looked around, slammed the door and strode to the desk. He elbowed Jason aside and said he wanted a room for tomorrow night. The clerk said he didn't have a room.

The man turned and glowered at Jason. "He get a room?" he said, pointing at Jason.

"He did," said the clerk, "the last one." The clerk smiled, sobered when he saw the rowdy's response.

The rowdy stared at Jason, eyes narrowed, turned back to the clerk. "You sure you ain't got a room for me? I want some comfort and a tub fulla hot water afore we head out."

"Sorry. No rooms till three nights out."

"That's too late."

"Sorry."

"Yeah, you need to be sorry." The rowdy spun on his heel and stormed out, slamming the door, causing

Jason and the clerk to start. They looked at each other.

Jason thanked the clerk and went out.

Jessie and the children sat on a short log beside the campfire. Christian poked the flames with a stick, stirring the embers, sending up a shower of sparks.

"Don't do that," said Jessie. "You'll burn the place down, too many things around here that can burn." He dropped the stick in the fire, crossed his arms and pouted. He shivered.

"I know, honey, it's cold, and it's boring, having nothing to do but wait. We're going to be on our way soon." She looked at the eastern horizon. "Look, the sun's coming, and it's going to warm up."

"I'm hungry, Mama," said Nicole.

Jessie reached over and hugged her. "So am I, sweetheart. Let's get some breakfast." Jessie stood and stretched, brightened. "Look, here comes Daddy!"

The children turned, saw Jason striding toward the wagon. They jumped up and ran to him. He touched each on the top of their heads, put his arms around their shoulders and walked toward the fire circle.

"Any news?" Jessie said.

"Lots of news! Word is that we leave day after tomorrow. Some men rode a few miles out yesterday. They found green grass everywhere, as far as they could see. They saw wildflowers. Bloodroot and Dutchmen's breeches, one said. I don't know them, but he said they were a sure sign of spring.

"That's what we've been waiting for, a break in the weather, sunshine and green grass. I'll be so glad to leave this place! I'm going to grow moss if we don't get moving. Six days in one place doing nothing but waiting is getting to me.

"But we're just about on our way. And that's not all." He grinned. "I booked us into the National Hotel for tomorrow night. We're going to have dinner in the café, take proper baths, and sleep in real beds. They said we could put the wagon and animals in the livery behind the hotel. There will be a couple of other wagons in there, and they'll put a guard on it."

The children beamed as he spoke and shouted at the end of his announcement. They hugged him around his waist, then hugged each other.

Jessie watched this uncharacteristic show of sibling affection, smiled at Jason. They watched the children walk away, hand in hand. They separated and bent to collect sticks for the fire.

Jessie put her arms around Jason's waist, and he encircled her shoulders.

"Are we really leaving?" she said.

"Yes, ma'am. As the boys in camp are saying: 'Ho for Oregon!'" A man nearby standing beside his wagon looked over at Jason's shout. The man smiled, waved.

Jason waved, turned back to Jessie. "By the way, we were lucky today. I got the last room." He told her about the ruckus at the hotel. "That old boy sounds like trouble."

He rubbed his stomach. "Now how about that breakfast I heard you announcing?"

Jessie and Jason and the two children sat at a linen-topped table in the National Hotel dining room. Jason pushed his chair back.

"That was a fine dinner, even if we didn't have anything to do with fixing it." Jessie smiled. Christian and Nicole continued scraping their bowls to get the last bit of apple cobbler.

"Now, I need to talk with a couple of old boys I met this morning about some trail stuff. We're meeting at Kelly's Watering Hole, the saloon down the street and around the corner. They are Santa Fe traders and said they could give me some pointers on what to expect on the trail. Should be helpful. Most of the men I've talked with in camp know no more about traveling on the plains than I do."

He stood and took his hat from the chair back. "When you're finished here, tell the clerk that you're ready for the bath, and he'll send the hot water up. If the water's not hot enough when it's my turn, I'll ask for another bucket." He bent and kissed Jessie on her cheek. He put his hands on the tops of the children's heads, leaned over and pecked each on a cheek.

"Bye, Daddy," said Nicole.

"Bye," Christian said. He waved with his spoon, scraped the bowl again.

Mother and children watched Jason as he walked through the door.

# Chapter 2

Jason paused on the hotel porch. The darkness was penetrated by slivers of light from draped and shuttered shops and houses on both sides of the street.

He inhaled deeply, exhaled. *Tomorrow it begins.* He smiled.

Stepping off the porch, he walked down the middle of the empty street. He had gone but a few steps when he heard a sharp cry from a dark alley between two buildings.

"No!" There it was again, followed by a mumbled curse, a different voice.

Jason walked slowly into the dark alley. He saw a man holding a short whip. The man raised the whip and struck the boy who cowered before him, holding his hands to his head.

"Here! What's going on here?" said Jason.

The man holding the whip turned sharply toward Jason. "Nothing that concerns you! Stay out of it!" He turned and struck the boy again with the whip.

Jason pulled up the bandanna around his neck to cover his face below his eyes. He grabbed the man's wrist that was raised to strike again, wrenched the whip from him. The man whirled around and swung at Jason. Jason brushed the fist aside and landed a right to the man's head. He crumpled to the ground and lay still.

Jason pulled the bandanna down. The boy lowered his hands from his head, watching Jason, still fearful, uncertain how to react. He couldn't have been more than fifteen or sixteen.

The boy, terrified, looked at his prostrate master. "He kill me now," softly.

Jason pondered. "No, he won't." The boy looked at him, waiting. "Do you know someplace you can hide for a while, maybe half an hour?"

The boy frowned, puzzled. "Yeah, the livery. A friend take care th' livery at night. His name Amos. He a free man."

"Go there and wait. I'll come for you in about a half hour."

"Yes, suh. Thank you, suh."

Jason stepped through the door of the saloon. He spotted the two Santa Fe traders and walked to their corner table. He extended his hand, and they shook. The two dark, bewhiskered men obviously had spent many seasons outdoors. They appeared to be in their sixties, though they might have been ten years younger.

"Andy. Paul," said Jason.

"Sit down," said Andy. He leaned back. "So you are about to launch out into the wilds for the great adventure." He smiled.

"I am indeed, and I appreciate your talking with me about it," said Jason. "Before we get to that, I need to ask you about something else. How do you feel about slavery?"

Paul and Andy frowned. "Where did that come from?" said Andy.

"I'll explain," said Jason. He waited.

"Well, I never owned a slave and never expect to," said Andy. "I don't cotton to owning a man like you own a beast."

Jason turned to Paul.

"That goes for me, too," Paul said.

"Good," said Jason. "I've got a problem. Well, not a problem, but something that needs fixing." He told them about the incident with the belligerent slave owner and the boy who was hiding at the livery.

"The boy said his owner surely would kill him now, so he needs to get away from this town fast. I wonder if you can help. I understand the Santa Fe traders get underway tomorrow."

"I know where you're going with this," said Paul, smiling.

"Yeah. Would you be able to get the boy in the caravan? You'd be saving his life."

"Hmm." Andy pondered. "Tell him this. Go to the campground tonight, and ask for Johnny D. Tell him to tell Johnny that Andy Milner sent him. Tell him to tell Johnny that I will come see him tonight soon as we finish here."

"Andy, you're a saint," said Jason. He stood. "I'll be right back." He strode to the door and went out.

In ten minutes, he returned and went to the corner table. He sat down and exhaled. "Right. It's done."

Andy, Paul and Jason leaned over their glasses, Jason's hardly touched while the glasses of the others were almost empty. Intense comment and belly laughs punctuated their animated conversation.

Paul leaned back. "I almost envy you. Almost. Me and Andy seen lots of country between here and Santa Fe. We saw good times and hard times. But that's over."

Jason frowned. "Over? I thought—"

"He cain't do it! By god, he cain't do it!" Jason and the two traders looked up abruptly at the shout. The speaker standing at the bar was the rowdy who had accosted the hotel clerk. The bartender said something to the man who pushed his empty glass across the counter. The bartender poured into the glass. The rowdy picked up the glass and took a long swallow. He shook his head.

"By god, he cain't do it" He weaved, raised the glass and emptied it. "He cain't do it," softly, staring into the empty glass. He pushed the glass across the counter, dug into a pocket and dumped some coins on the countertop. He turned, blinked and shook his head, then shuffled, weaving and stumbling, across the room. He leaned against the outside door until it opened, and he went through. The door closed behind him.

"That old boy's got a snootful," said Paul. "Sure wouldn't want to be following him tomorrow. He might take a left turn and head for Texas." Andy waved to the bartender who walked over with a bottle. He poured into the traders' glasses. Jason held up a hand, palm outward. The bartender nodded and walked back to the bar.

The crowd and din in the saloon had increased considerably the past hour. "Looks like everbody is toasting the leaving," said Andy. "Kelly'll hate to see 'em go. This place'll be empty tomorrow night."

"Well, I won't be here to confirm that," said Jason. He pushed his glass a few inches on the table. "Now, I've taken up far too much of your time, my friends. And my bath water is cold by now. You've probably noticed that I need a bath."

Paul leaned over, sniffed, wrinkled his nose, leaned back. Both of the traders laughed. "Nothing new there. By the time you reach Oregon, you'll thank everbody smells like roses."

At that moment, the outside door burst open. A wild-eyed man stood in the doorway.

"Fire!"

Everyone in the room rushed to the door, jostling, pushing. Jason squeezed through and ran to the center of the street. He looked both ways, saw the glow at the corner and ran in that direction. Rounding the corner, he stopped.

*The hotel!*

He ran down the street, dodging others, confused, running in all directions. People stopped to gape, hands on heads, groaning, what to do, what to do?

Jason stopped in front of the hotel. The entire front wall of the two-story structure was a sheet of flames, soaring, crackling and groaning in the light breeze. He ran toward the entrance until others grabbed him and pulled him back from the conflagration.

He looked wildly around at the crowd of terrified people, searching. He ran to a knot of bystanders, questioned them—have you seen a woman and two children, a boy and a girl?—then ran to another, and another, repeating his desperate question. Have you seen my family? Anybody? Help me! They shook their heads, mumbled their condolences. Sorry, old man; sorry, my friend.

"The back door!" shouted a man. He ran to the side of the hotel, Jason and another on his heels. They had hardly reached the building's side when an explosion behind the hotel blew the lead runner off his feet. Jason and the other man helped him up, and they scrambled back toward the street as a fireball rose from the hotel's rear.

"What was that?" said the man who had been downed by the blast, his clothes in tatters.

"Oh, my," said a bystander. "That's the gunpowder that was stored in the shed by the livery."

*The livery. The wagon and animals are gone.*

"Buckets!" shouted someone behind him. Two men carrying half a dozen empty buckets each ran up, dumped the buckets on the ground. "Get water in the troughs!" Men and women grabbed buckets and ran to watering troughs where terrified horses were tied, bucking, pulling on reins until some snapped, and people dodged the escaping, galloping horses. A woman untied the other horses and slapped their sides, sending them off.

Men and women dipped buckets in troughs and ran to the fire, threw the water on the flames, ran back for more water. The water in the troughs was quickly exhausted, and they stood with empty, dripping buckets, watching the flames.

Jason dropped his bucket, collapsed to his knees. He could only watch as his life ebbed, vanishing in the flames. He groaned, clenched his eyes. *Jessie. Christian. Nicole. I can't see them.*

He turned aside at a shout.

"I told yuh, by god! I said he cain't do it! I got him, by god!" It was the rowdy, weaving, his eyes glazed. He stood behind the people who now turned and looked at him.

Jason, still on his knees, tears streaming down his face, saw him. Jason rose slowly, made his way through the throng until he stood before the grinning man.

"You did this?" Jason said softly.

"Yeah, by damn! I told him! I—"

The rowdy was lifted off his feet by Jason's blow to the stomach. The man bent forward, crumpling. Jason grabbed an arm, lifted and struck him a crushing blow to the head with the other fist. The rowdy collapsed to the ground. Jason shouted, a primitive howl, and kicked him hard in his side, grunting with the effort. He kicked again, a glancing blow to the head. Jason bent over the prostrate figure, gasping, sobbing.

The crowd that had been drawn to the beating drifted away. Two men stayed and took Jason gently by the arms, led him away. Jason did not resist. He was limp, spent, a body without life. The men guided him to a bench where he collapsed, his hands covering his face.

*I'm dead. What does a dead man do when he knows he's dead?*

"My friend." Jason opened his eyes to slits, turned to see Paul, the Santa Fe trader, sitting beside him. Andy stood nearby.

Jason closed his eyes, lowered his head, turned his head slowly, side to side.

"The man is dead," Paul said. "Nobody here seems to know him, but surely there's somebody in camp knows him. There could be trouble."

Jason looked aside at Paul, his eyes glazed, his cheeks marked with tear tracks.

"Most people who know what he did will thank you for killing the sumbitch, but some will figure you had no right to take a life, something only the authorities should do. Some might say that he was drunk and didn't know what he was doing. Some who knew him might say he was a simple-minded man, a good man when he wasn't riled or drunk. Don't chance it. You need to think about gettin' away from here."

Jason looked at the burning hotel. The top floor was gone, and the flames burned lower. There was little else to burn.

"That's where I need to go," Jason said softly.

Paul looked up at Andy. He cocked his head. After a moment, Andy nodded.

"Look. Me and Andy are leaving at first light tomorrow for New Orleans. Go with us. Stay with us at our camp tonight. The authorities ain't going to be too anxious to find out who did this. Not tonight, at least. We'll be gone before they get serious about looking tomorrow. How 'bout it?"

Jason looked down at his feet. He nodded.

Jason heard a fluttering and looked up. The sails flapped lightly and began to fill. The ship leaned ever so slightly to starboard. The breeze quickened, filling the sails, and the ship heeled over. He looked over the side and saw a bow wake. The ship was underway.

Stamping sounds came from below, and people burst from the stairwells. Crewmen ran to their stations, and passengers went to rails. They looked up at sails and over the side at the wake, rolling away from the bow. A cheer rose from the throng.

Jason stared at the horizon. He closed his eyes, felt the breeze on his hot cheeks and neck. He had a fleeting impulse to smile until he remembered that he was alone, and he would never see his family again. He would never smile again. He lowered his head and choked on a sob.

"Okay, old man?" said Paul. He leaned on the rail. Jason had not heard him come up.

Jason looked up at Paul, his face blank. He turned and stared at the horizon.

The following wind picked up, and the ship plowed ahead in a choppy sea. “Making headway finally,” said Andy. “Best breeze since leaving New Orleans.”

Jason looked aside, nodded to Paul, looked back at the horizon. He turned, walked to the stairwell, nodded to Andy who was climbing the stair, and went down.

Andy watched him go, turned and walked to Paul at the rail. He shook his head, stared at the horizon. “That poor man is not in a boat in the Caribbean. He’s in hell.”

A movement ahead caught his eye. “Look,” he said to Paul. A single bird, a large blue-gray bird with a white head, flew high across the bow.

They looked beyond the bow toward the horizon, straining for the first glimpse of land. The black line that was the horizon took on texture and dimples that gradually lifted and became trees and mountains.

Panama.

# Chapter 3

Jason, Paul and Andy stood on the dock at Chagres, packs at their feet. They looked around at a tropical landscape of palms and ferns and other plants that were strange to Jason.

They hefted their packs and walked down the wharf. Knots of Americans, all men, stood on the wharf and in roads that led from the wharf into the town. Smoking and chatting, the Americans eyed the three newcomers with glances that suggested curiosity or suspicion, or both.

Extending from the wharf inland, the town was a collection of hundreds of huts made of bamboo poles, roofs covered with palm leaves. Just off the wharf, a single wood frame house was fronted by a rough sign that named the establishment Crescent City and offered accommodation.

They walked on. Some of the huts doubled as shops where an assortment of local products was offered: coconuts, cocoa, oranges, bananas, plantains, rum and brandy, sweet cakes.

They stopped at a table displaying fruits and vegetables and an array of bottles of varying colors and sizes. The owner, sitting on a stool behind the table, smiled. Paul picked up a bottle of spirits, examined it and replaced it on the bench. He wrinkled his nose, turning to the others. "I intend to stay away from anything in this place that I cain't peel or crack open."

A man dressed in white trousers and coat walked on the dock in their direction. He glanced casually at the three strangers.

*"Amigo!"* Andy called. The man stopped, and Andy walked to him. Jason was surprised to hear a spirited conversation in Spanish. He turned to Paul, frowning.

Paul smiled. "Helps to know the language so you know whether the other side's cheating you. Anybody in the Santa Fe trade picks it up pretty early. Spanish is easy. You'll probably be fluent before we reach the Pacific coast."

Andy thanked the man and walked back to his compatriots. The man strolled on, turned and looked at the three over his shoulder.

"It's just down the way here," said Andy. He pointed. "The outfitter there runs parties across to the other side. He said there's a passel leaving tomorrow morning. I don't see any reason to hang around this place, so I think we should try to get in that bunch. We won't need to find a room or even pitch a tent, not in this weather. How does that sound?" The others nodded.

They walked off the wharf to a dusty street lined on both sides with what appeared to be adobe walls that fronted shops and houses. They stopped at an open door in a wall. Andy walked inside, leaving the others standing in the street. After a few minutes, he reappeared.

"Okay, we meet the outfitter and members of the party right here tomorrow morning at 8:00. Had to pay a few dollars extra to get on that boat. Most people trying to get to the other side wait days before finding passage. Least, that's what the outfitter said. He said he's busy, all right, but it's nothing like last year.

"He said the people that come through here last year—he called 'em the 49ers—was shoulder to shoulder, yelling for a seat on the next boat and sometimes getting into scuffles to make their point. One time, he said, there was a thousand here at one time, trying to buy passage. Nothing like that this year, but I think he was right happy to take my bribe to put us on tomorrow's boat. Hope we don't meet the fellars who he bumped off to accommodate us.

"Now, let's test the local brew." He beckoned, and they walked back the way they came and turned down a side street.

Rounding the corner, they stopped almost immediately and stepped aside at the approach of a procession. Two Americans walked beside a wagon drawn by a team of shuffling mules that raised little puffs of dust on the dirt road. A rough wooden casket lay in the bed. A dozen locals followed the Americans. As the procession passed, Andy stepped out and walked beside a barefoot priest in a long black robe. They talked softly in Spanish. After a bit, Andy nodded to him and returned to Jason and Paul.

"He was a doctor from Ohio," Andy said. "Gave up everything, family, position, prospects, bitten by the gold bug. The padre said this was the third burial in three days. 'This country is tough on soft foreigners,' he said. He smiled, damn him."

Andy looked up into the tops of the forest of palms and fig trees. "I wonder who will be next."

As if in answer, they stared silently across the river at the remains of a squalid encampment of tents and board hovels that had housed a multitude of Americans last year. They had arrived in Chagres just months after the announcement of the gold discoveries in California's Sierra Nevada. They had descended on the town before Panamanians were prepared to house, feed and transport these Argonauts bound for the Pacific. In such crowded, unsanitary conditions, sickness and disease were inevitable. Crewmen on their ship had told them about the pestilential encampment and warned them to stay clear.

They walked on and stopped at a cantina in the wall. Paul and Jason pulled out chairs at one of the two outside tables and sat down while Andy went inside. He returned, followed by a bartender carrying a tray holding three full glasses. The bartender set the drinks on the table, nodded, went back inside.

Andy sat down, picked up his glass. He wiped the rim with his sleeve, raised the glass. *"Salud."*

The others picked up their drinks, followed Andy's example and wiped the glasses, and all sipped.

"Well, it sounds like it's gonna be easy going, not what I expected," said Andy. "We take a boat for a few days as far upriver as the boat can go, then we rent passage on mules for a ride of a day or two to the Pacific. Sounds like fun."

Jason, Paul and Andy stood with a group of two dozen others on the bank of the river, bags at their feet, staring at canoes attached to the shore by short lines. The outfitter talked with a couple of men at the edge of the group.

The boats were strange craft the outfitter called *cayucas.* They were hollowed out logs, about twenty-five feet long, each topped with a palm leaf canopy. Three or four crewmen sat in each of the canoes, looking expectantly at their prospective passengers.

"We're getting in that?" said Paul.

"Perfectly seaworthy, I'm told," said Andy. "Yeah, I know they don't much look like canoes, but the outfitter said they're stable and ride like a big ship. Except when they capsize." He grinned. "They carry bananas from Las Cruces, about forty-five miles up river, dump the bananas here in Chagres, then carry chumps like us back to Las Cruces. The alternative is to walk through the jungle, and nobody recommends that. Either the wildlife eats you, or the bandits beat you up and rob you. I'm told the mosquitoes is so big, you have to protect yourself with a machete. I'll take the canoe."

"Sounds good to me," said Paul. He and Andy looked at Jason. "Jason?" Paul said.

"Okay by me".

"All aboard," Andy said. "That's ours." He pointed at the canoe tied up a few steps away. The three crewmen, who had listened to all this and saw Andy point, smiled. One waved.

"Let's get our gear aboard, and we're on our way," Andy said.

They shouldered their bags and stepped to the edge of the bank. Handing his bag to a crewman, Paul ducked under the palm leaf canopy, started to step aboard, wavered, grasped the outstretched hand of a boatman, and stepped gingerly into the canoe. The canoe rocked gently, side to side.

The crewman motioned for Paul to sit on the last bench at the back. Another boatman squatted in the stern behind the bench, his hand resting on the tiller.

Andy and Jason followed, taking the proffered hand and stepping carefully into the center of the canoe. Jason sat beside Paul, Andy on the bench in front of them.

"Okay, let's get underway," said Paul. The boatmen looked blankly at Paul.

Paul spoke in Spanish to the boatman who sat in the bow along with another boatman. The man turned around, smiled, pointed at some men standing on the bank.

The outfitter stepped from the group, beckoning two men to come with him. He walked on the bank to the canoe where Jason and the traders watched all this. The outfitter turned to the two Americans with him and pointed at the canoe. The two men frowned, looked at each other.

"That boat's taken," said one of the Americans in English to the outfitter.

The outfitter replied in English. "The boat can take six passengers. There'll be five in this boat. You are lucky."

The American looked at Jason, Paul and Andy who had listened to the exchange. "I want another boat, for us two."

"Sure, I can do that. You paid fifteen dollars each for a place on this boat. If you want your own boat, the price is fifty dollars each for the two of you, and I won't have a boat for you until next week."

"No, goddammit, that won't do!"

The outfitter glanced aside at two burly rough-dressed men with bristly beards who had listened to this exchange. One of them removed the cigarro from his mouth and tossed it into the river. The two took a couple of steps toward their patron and his belligerent customer.

The American glanced at his partner, mumbled under his breath. Picking up his pack, he walked to the boat and tossed the pack aboard, almost hitting Andy.

"Easy does it, compatriot," said Andy. "You're making an ass of yourself."

The man stiffened, glared at Andy. "I ain't your compatriot, and I'll take care of myself and you too, if that's what you want."

Andy turned around, smiled at Paul and Jason. Andy looked up at his antagonist, patted the bench beside him. "Why don't you take this seat right here beside me, and we'll talk about your problem."

The outfitter glared at the two Americans on the dock. "By god, that'll do. We're wasting time! If you're not satisfied with my services, then get away from my boat, and you can walk to Cruces. And good luck with that. What's it gonna be? This canoe needs to leave, with you or with some of those folks standing on the bank, listening to this drivel." He motioned to a huddled crowd nearby, packs on backs or at their feet, looking anxiously at the boats and the outfitter.

The two Americans boarded slowly, ignoring the proffered hand of the boatman. Both sat on the bench in front of Andy.

The outfitter said something in Spanish to the three boatmen. They picked up their paddles, pushed off from the shore, dipped paddles into the water and pulled hard. The crewman in the stern touched the tiller lightly, turning into the stream.

They were underway. Jason looked at the soft bow wake as the men stroked in unison. He peered down at the water that appeared to flow past the side of the canoe.

The boat was soon in midstream and alone. It was the first canoe to pull away from the dock that morning. After rounding a bend, there was only the river and the forest.

Trees on each side of the river were choked with vines and a profusion of brightly colored blossoms. Birds of every hue flew about the branches, and their songs filled the forest. Lime trees were heavy with fruit. Small neatly cultivated patches of corn and other vegetables occasionally broke the wall of foliage. Sugar cane grew in the patches and in the wild.

Scattered wild turkeys foraged at the edge of the forest. Small alligators sunned on the bank and slid into the water at the approach of the canoe.

As they watched, a large animal emerged from the dense growth on the bank and watched the boat. It was as large as a small horse, dark brown with a head that appeared a cross between a pig and a mule with an abbreviated snout that suggested a kinship with elephants.

"What the hell is that?" said Paul.

"Dunno," Andy said, "strange looking beast." He said something in Spanish over his shoulder to the boatman behind him. He turned back to the front. "He said the English word is 'tapir.' Never heard of it."

The tapir's head suddenly jerked up, and the animal whirled and vanished noiselessly into the dark jungle. A flash of yellow crossed a sunny spot where the tapir disappeared.

"Jaguar!" a boatman in the bow shouted. He unleashed a flurry of Spanish directed at Andy.

"He says they don't see jaguar often in daytime. He said that one must be real hungry and shouldn't have any trouble downing the tapir."

They searched the foliage where the tapir had disappeared, but saw no more movement. Looking back to the front, Jason watched the bow ripples in the flat stream flow slowly from the boat toward the bank. But for occasional birdcalls, the only distraction was the soft, rhythmic sounds of paddles dipping into the green water, drops falling from paddle tips into the languid flow.

*****

Jason jerked upright. He had been dozing and was awakened when the canoe nudged the bank. A boatman in the bow crawled over the side into the shallows and tied the boat's line to a bush that projected over the water. The other two crewmen jumped over the side and began splashing about in the waist deep stream. They wore only light shirts and loose short pants.

Jason looked around. No other boats were in sight. The stream was almost dead calm, with only a gentle current. No sounds broke the silence but the splashing of the boatmen. Jason's head came up at the call of an unseen bird in the canopy. He looked up for the singer, saw no movement but the gentle swaying of the treetops.

"Black-faced Solitaire!" said a boatman standing in the shallows beside the canoe. He grinned. He spoke rapidly to Andy in Spanish.

"An American translated the Spanish for him," said Andy. "He sounds pretty proud of hisself."

"What th' hell's this all about!" said the troublesome passenger, still sitting in front of Andy. He glared at the boatmen, splashing in the shallows. "Little Grump," Andy had named him.

He had named Grump's partner, "Stump," because, Andy said, he seems to just sit quietly, cut off from the world, doing nothing useful. At this pronouncement, Paul had called Andy a "goddam philosopher."

"Looks to me like the locals know how to cool off," said Andy.

Americans for the most part, arriving in Panama in winter or spring, wore heavy clothing. Most had no room in their bags for changes of light clothes. So they either bore up under the humid heat, or they shed clothing.

Paul had started shedding clothing when he saw what the boatmen were about. "Looks like a damn good idea to me," said Paul. Now he was stark naked and eased over the side of the boat into the cooling, green water. "Ahhh."

"By god!" said Little Grump. "This is disgusting!"

Jason sat quietly, staring into the canopy.

Three canoes were tied to stakes in the bank before a rough structure the outfitter in Chagres had described as a café-hotel. Andy and Paul agreed that it was unlike any café-hotel they had ever seen. It had the appearance of a large cylindrical box, unpainted and unkempt. Tall ceiba trees towered over the café and along the bank.

Inside, passengers sat at four tables. Others sat at three tables outside and lounged about the bank. Some smoked, others drank coffee or a vile-looking brandy.

Jason sat with Paul at an inside table near a window. Empty plates and serving bowls were stacked in the center of the table. They held mugs of coffee. Andy walked in from outside, pulled out a chair and sat down.

"What did we just eat, Andy?" said Paul.

Andy grinned. "Kinda tasted like chicken, didn't it? Well, it weren't. I have it on good authority that we just ate iguana. The good authority I refer to is that sweet little señorita over there." He pointed toward the kitchen door. "I talked with her out back just now. Well, I say I talked." He grinned. She looked at him, head lowered, smiling.

"She's got the softest little bee-hind and sweetest mouth I tasted in a long time." Paul snickered. Jason turned and looked through the front door.

Andy noticed. "Jason, old friend. I'm sorry. I cain't pretend to understand what you're going through. But man, you gotta keep living. I think your wife would want you to keep living."

Jason turned back to the table.

"Sorry, it's none of my business," said Andy, "but I like you. We like you, and we want to see you pull through this. We got something to look forward to. The three of us. We're gonna dig us a barrel of gold and be king uh th' mountain."

Jason stared into his coffee cup, raised his chin and tried to smile, without success. "Sorry to be so . . . so dark. You've been good friends. You probably saved my life. I'm not sure yet whether to thank you for that." He raised his hand, palm outward, to stifle their protests. "I know you meant this trip to be happy. Satisfying, at least.

"Tell me what you plan to do. All I know is that you two got bit bad by the gold bug."

Paul and Andy exchanged glances. "Well, you got it right at the start, old friend," said Paul. "We was pretty happy with the Santa Fe trade, but when we heard about the gold discovery in California, we was hooked. Not just for the money, although we do like money, but for the fun. Hell, we're gonna have fun while gettin' rich! How can you beat that?"

"We plan on buying an outfit in San Francisco and head for the mountains," Andy said. "We'll learn as we go. Maybe we'll need to partner with somebody who knows what he's doing till we can strike out on our own. We don't cotton to no long-term associations."

Jason frowned, looked aside.

"Not you!" said Paul. "You're one of us now, for as long as you want to be." Paul clapped Jason on the shoulder.

"Hey! You!" It was Little Grump. He and Stump sat at a table near the door. He motioned for the serving girl to come to his table, the same *señorita* Andy had flirted with out behind the cafe. She darted a glance at Andy, walked to Grump's table.

"This coffee is terrible! More sugar!" The girl frowned, frightened. She stole a glance at Andy.

*"Azúcar, mi angelita"* Andy said softly. She smiled, ducked her head, looked at Grump, then back at Andy. She took Grump's cup and walked to the open door of the kitchen. Grump glared at Andy.

In the kitchen doorway, the girl picked up a short piece of sugar cane from a bin, bit off a mouthful from the end. She vigorously chewed the chunk. Walking back to Grump's table, she spat the sugary liquid into the cup, set the cup on the table.

Grump had watched this, open-mouthed and wide-eyed. He stared down at the cup.

"What the hell! You dammed bitch!" He stood, grabbed her arms and shook her. She was surprised, terror on her face.

Andy and Paul started to stand. Jason stood slowly, held out a hand to stop Andy and Paul. He walked to Grump's table, stopped behind him.

"Let her go," Jason said softly.

Grump turned his head to face Jason, still holding the girl. "Stay out of this, you spineless prick!"

Jason grabbed Grump tightly around the back of his neck, squeezed. "Let her go," he said, softly. He tightened his grip on his neck. Grump tried to pull away, wheezing.

Grump's partner, Stump, stood and reached for Jason. Jason pushed him hard in the chest with his free hand, sending him crashing against his chair. The chair shattered, and he sprawled. Everyone in the café looked around for the ruckus.

Grump gurgled and released the girl. Jason turned Grump around and walked him to the outside door. When they were through the door, Jason released his hold on his neck and pushed him.

Grump stumbled, turned around, rubbing the side of his neck. "This is not over, you son of a bitch."

Jason stood where he was until Grump turned and walked toward the river, still rubbing his neck. Stump scurried around Jason, watching him as he passed.

Jason walked back inside and sat down at the table. Paul and Andy grinned broadly.

"The funny part," said Andy," is that I watched her put sugar in my coffee the same way, out back. Hell, I didn't mind. Come to think of it, that's the reason for her sweet mouth."

# Chapter 4

After the stop for lunch at the café, the voyage resumed. Following a half hour of smooth sailing, the canoe went aground repeatedly on the sandy bottom. Boatmen crawled over the side, rocked the canoe off the bar until it floated, climbed back in and commenced paddling. Until the boat grounded again.

Now the canoe glided up to a small wharf. Giant ceiba and kapok and Panama trees towered over the landing and a scattering of huts and a few adobe and stone houses. The boatman in the bow stepped up on the wharf and tied the line to a pole. He motioned to Andy to come ashore.

"Now what!" Grump was not pleased.

The boatman and Andy talked as the other passengers debarked and stood aside, waiting. Andy walked over to the others.

"Okay, folks, here it is. The river is too shallow to go up any further. This here is Gorgona, motioning toward the huts and other nondescript structures. We're five miles from Cruces."

"So how do we get there?" said Grump, glaring at Andy.

"We walk. They don't have any animals for us, but we can hire some men to help carry our bags and guide us. I'm told the trail through the forest is pretty narrow and rough in places. Unless there's people ahead of us beating it down, I'm told the trail can just about disappear in places. That's why we need to buy us a guide."

"The hell we do!" Grump said. "I'm not paying anybody! We paid for transport to Las Cruces. They need to get us and our packs there!"

"Good luck with that," said Andy. "In the wet season, the boats can go all the way. But this ain't the wet season." He turned to Jason and Paul. "Let's get our gear and see if we can hire a couple of locals to carry and guide. We can pitch a tent here on the bank if we need to and be off first thing tomorrow morning."

The three hefted their packs and walked to the outskirts of the town, leaving Grump and Stump standing on the bank, Grump fuming and Stump staring blankly.

First light. A faint glow in the east outlined the dense canopy of Panama trees with their fan-like roots radiating from the foot of the trunk. Thin palms pierced the canopy, fronds swaying gently.

Andy, Paul and Jason, kneeling at their rough camp on the bank, stuffed blankets into packs. Andy stood, saw four locals walk up and stop nearby. One waved to him. He walked over and huddled with them. Andy gestured toward Grump and Stump who were rolled in their blankets in a grassy spot on the bank.

Andy walked down the bank. He kicked Grump's foot. Grump jumped and sat bolt upright, wide-eyed.

"Wha—"

"Your packers are here. We're leaving in five minutes. It might be wise to walk together. Word is this trail can be a bit dangerous. You don't want to walk it alone." Grump and Stump rolled out of their blankets and began furiously packing.

Andy walked back to his camp, smiling.

"What?" said Paul.

"Just told Grump and Stump that they're in danger of getting waylaid on the trail if they don't get their asses up and rolling and walk with us."

"Is that true?" said Paul.

"Nah, just having a little fun."

Paul gestured with a nod of his head toward Jason. He stood on the bank, staring at the stream, watching the leaves and small branches floating below in the languid current. He lowered his head, eyes closed, wiped his eyes with a sleeve.

Andy frowned at Paul, shook his head. "Jason," Andy called. "Need to pack up, old friend. Gotta get on our way."

Jason turned, walked slowly to the camp. He knelt and finished stuffing his blanket into the bag.

Their packing finished, Andy waved to the four locals. Two headed for Andy's camp, and the other two walked to Grump and Stump. The locals hefted packs and bags, adjusted them on their backs and shoulders and set out toward an opening in the rainforest.

Andy hurried after them and beckoned for the others to follow. "Come on! We don't want to lose these guys. *Vamonos!*" Over his shoulder, "that's 'let's go' for you *norteamericanos.*"

Paul guffawed.

Single-file, they stepped into the opening in the dense forest wall and disappeared.

"Damn, it's winter, supposed to be cold," said Paul. He wiped his face with a bandanna, stuffed it into a pocket.

"You ain't in Santa Fe, *amigo*," said Andy.

"Yeah, there's that. I sure hope we ain't still here in summer."

"Yeah, closed in like this, th' damned trail is like an oven. Won't be long. The lead packer said we're about half way to the main road where we should be able to rent passage on animals."

Grump and Stump, anxious at the beginning, had fallen in close behind their two packers. Grump plodded along, his head down, grumbling. Stump carried a stout stick, alternately using it for a walking stick of sorts and striking foliage alongside the trail, annoying all around him.

Paul and Andy followed them, with the two other packers behind Andy. Jason lagged ten yards behind the last packer. He shuffled, head down, oblivious to the forest and occasional bird calls and conversation of the others.

Andy and Paul had tried to cheer Jason ever since leaving Independence, to give him something to think about besides the tragedy that weighed him down and threatened to drown him in sorrow.

Jason had wanted to respond, somehow to express his appreciation for their concern. But he could not. He was still numb, overcome with guilt. He was alive, and they were not. He should have been there at the hotel to lead his family from the inferno. He should have saved them. He could have done *something* to save them. But he did not, and he could not shake the conviction that he was doomed. He feared he could not live with the guilt. He could not come to grips with the prospect of a life without them.

Jason's head jerked up at a shout. Two strangers stood in the trail ahead, facing the lead porters. Their dress identified them as locals. The long knife that one held before him identified them as bandits. Jason could not understand the barrage of Spanish, but the porters understood. They dropped their loads and vanished into the forest.

Jason whirled around and saw three other brigands. Two brandished knives. Jason turned back to the front at a sharp gunshot. The bandit with the knife was blown backward, dropping the blade. Grump held a pistol, still pointed at the fallen man. At the same time, Stump had attacked the other man with the heavy, short stick he carried. He connected to the side of the head and again to his neck, then his side. The thug was more surprised than hurt, and he charged Stump. Grump turned from the downed man and struck the other repeatedly with the pistol. The assailant decided this was a bad bargain and retreated into the forest.

At the rear, Paul and Andy had sized up the situation in an instant. Their eyes fixed on the bandits, they bent and slowly pulled long skinning knives from boot scabbards, pushed past Jason to confront the three bandits. Andy grinned.

The three looked at each other and stepped backwards, then turned and ran off the trail, disappearing into the forest.

"Well, that was a little excitement on a dull day," said Paul. He and Andy pushed knives into scabbards.

Grump was not amused. He stared at Jason. "You . . . I'm fed up with your attitude! You just stood there like a bump on a log, watching us deal with the bandits. "

"Easy," said Paul. "He's had to deal with more serious stuff than some amateur bandits."

"No, I won't go easy. He stood by and let us save his sorry ass."

Andy spoke softly. "He lost his family, Grump. He's still grieving."

Grump advanced on Jason, pushed him in the chest. Jason retreated a step, looked blankly at Grump.

Paul stepped toward Grump. Andy held up a hand to stop him, a smile playing about his lips. Paul looked at him, questioning. Andy nodded toward the two antagonists.

Grump leaned into Jason's face. "So you lost your family, so they're not here. They probably kicked your sorry ass out and are glad to be rid of yuh. So now—"

Grump was thrown sideways by Jason's blow to his jaw. Before he could fall, Jason grabbed him by an arm and smashed him on the other side of his face. Grump collapsed to the ground. He did not move, his eyes closed, jaw hanging.

Andy turned to Stump. "He's all yours, *amigo*. We're on our way." He and Paul and Jason collected their packs and hefted them onto their backs.

Stump watched, open-mouthed. "Wait! What if they come back?" he stammered.

"Then you got a problem," Andy said.

The three partners moved off, Jason rubbing his fist. Just before rounding a bend in the trail, Jason looked back to see Stump frantically shaking Grump, slapping his face, moving his head side to side. Stump looked up, terrified, saw Jason. Then they were gone.

Paul, Andy and Jason plodded along on the trail, leaning forward to counter the weight of the packs that had become heavier with every step. Paul mopped his face and neck with a bandanna. Huge trees leaned over the trail, but the high humidity of the rainforest nullified any comfort provided by the shade.

Andy stopped, shrugged his pack off, lowered it to the ground. “Stop for a bite.” Paul and Jason slid their packs from their shoulders. They sat down heavily, dug into packs and pulled out cloth bundles of bread and chunks of beef they had packed at Gorgona.

They ate in silence, breathing deeply, drinking water from canteens, looking up at the forest canopy and the cloudless blue sky.

When they were finished, Andy pushed food cloths and canteen into his pack. He stood, picked up the pack and swung it to his shoulders. “Time to go, *amigos*. We’ll not get rich settin’ here.” Paul and Jason closed their packs, stood, reached for their pack straps.

“Wait. Please. Wait.” A faint, anguished shout.

They stopped, hands on packs, stared at the back trail, searching, saw only the forest. They looked at each other.

“Well?” said Andy.

“Let’s wait,” Jason said.

Hands still on packs, they stared at the back trail where it emerged from the heavy cover. Stump appeared first. He carried a pack on his back and dragged another, occasionally bending to pull with both hands. Grump shuffled behind Stump, head down, blood dripping from his open mouth.

Coming up to the three, Stump dropped the straps of the pack he was dragging. He struggled to remove the pack from his back and dropped it heavily to the ground. He bent over, hands on knees, gasping. Grump glanced abruptly at the three partners, knelt and collapsed to all fours, inhaling heavily.

"Thanks, boys, thanks," said Stump between gasps. "If you'll just give us a minute, we'll keep up. Thanks."

The three waited, looking around at the forest, listening to birdcalls, watching the thin limbs in the canopy wave gently.

Jason watched Stump and Grump. He opened his pack, reached in, pulled the canteen out and offered it to Stump. Stump looked up, surprised. He took the canteen, drank, handed it to his partner. Grump took it and drank in long swallows, water trickling down his chin. He wiped his mouth, offered it to Jason without looking at him. Jason took it and pushed it into his pack.

"We need to get moving," said Andy. "I still think we can get to Panama City today. If we can hire animals to transport us." Andy and Paul shouldered their packs and stepped off.

Stump looked up, alarmed. He picked up his pack, grunting with the effort as he swung it to his back. He grasped the straps of Grump's pack and tried to lift it, wheezing, straining. He gave up, bent over the pack and choked back a sob.

Jason shouldered his pack. He reached down and took the straps of the pack at Stump's feet. He lifted it to his other shoulder and set out. Stump, open-mouthed, watched Jason move off behind Paul and Andy. Stump adjusted the pack on his back and followed Jason.

Grump struggled up and fell in behind Stump.

Trudging through a particularly dense copse, the five walkers started when the forest opened to a wide corridor in the heavy rainforest. A rough paved road ran down the middle of the corridor.

"Be damned," said Paul. "Would yuh look at this?"

They stared at a road laid with stone. They had heard at Chagres about the road, paved centuries ago by the Spanish. It had been neglected for decades, but the stone surface was still adequate for most of its length for sure-footed mules. So Andy had been told. Except there were no animals in sight.

Andy rubbed his face with both hands. "According to the word back at Gorgona, it's about fifteen miles to Panama. We could walk it, but I was really looking forward to riding." He arched his back. "Oh, my back hurts somethin' terrible."

He grimaced, looked at the stone road that led westward to Panama City. In the other direction from this junction, the road ran a few miles back to Las Cruces.

"What to do?" Andy said. "I sure don't want to carry this confounded pack fifteen more miles, and I don't particularly want to walk back to Cruces to get animals. I sure do hate to backtrack and—"

His head came up at a shrill sound from the forest in the Panama City direction. He stared at the opening where the track disappeared into the trees and heavy undergrowth. There it was again, an elongated sound that was a combination cough, a series of sneezes and an anguished yell.

Andy grinned. "If I'm not dreaming, there's a good ol' Missouri mule on that road coming our way!"

At that moment, a cluster of mules and a single donkey emerged from the forest on the road. Riders were astride the two mules at the front, and the other animals were on leads.

Andy waved to the riders and walked to the road. When they came up to him, they stopped. An animated conversation in Spanish followed. Andy walked back to his companions.

"This fella says that he really wants to go on to Cruces and rest. But I convinced him that what he really needs to do is take us to Panama City and rest later with a few more coins in his pocket. He said he needs an hour to feed and water his animals and hisself, then we're off."

The ride through the rainforest on the stone-surfaced road was a lark. At least, for four of the riders, it was a lark. Stump joined in conversation and smiled often, even laughed once. He introduced himself as "Michael, Mike, as you like," grinning. Grump, last in the cavalcade, rode head down, gloomy. He said nothing.

The leafy cathedral they rode through seemed to stifle conversation. But for the sun's rays that filtered through the limbs stretching over the trail, the rainforest was dense and dark. Cecropia, trumpet trees, bore large clusters of broad leaves, shutting out the light. The trunk of the gumbo limbo tree was covered with a paper-thin outer covering which peeled off to reveal a bright green bark. Huge guanacaste trees, whose trunk diameter could reach six feet, pierced the canopy. The parasitic strangler fig clung to the trunk of many of these, enveloping it, stealing its vitality, and eventually strangling it.

The muleteers, who seemed immune to the beauty and majesty of the rainforest, became more animated when the mule caravan left the forest and entered the outskirts of Panama City. The leader of the group, riding beside Andy, said that no ships bound for California had called in Panama City in three weeks, so all the hotels were full. The overflow was camped in open spots in and around the town.

Andy asked the guides if camping in these spots was safe. The muleteers were unimpressed, perhaps offended at the question. They assured him that theft was unknown until the Americans arrived, and it was the Americans that stole. From each other. The guide laughed when he said this, but he assured Andy that it was true. Andy said nothing of the attempted robbery by locals on the trail from Gorgona.

Andy and the others decided that camping suited them fine. They stopped in a park and looked around for a likely place to camp. Why pay for accommodation when they could squat here in comfort? Grump did not take part in the discussion. He stood on the edge of the group, staring blankly at the ocean.

After setting up a rough camp, the four, minus Grump, strolled into the fringes of the town. For safety, they carried their packs, lightened by non-essential items like blankets and cooking gear that they could afford to lose to thieves.

Upon leaving the park, they walked through extensive ruins of large buildings that once had been grand estates dating from the Spanish era. Poor huts inhabited mostly by black people were scattered among the ruins. Beyond, stone and brick houses and commercial structures were covered with tiles, plastered and whitewashed. They were mostly three stories, with balconies that extended over walkways. Streets were paved, and most were bordered with sidewalks.

They walked through an open-air market that offered a great variety of fruits and vegetables. Slabs and slices of pork and beef were displayed, as well as live chickens. The presence of Americans sent prices soaring last year, the first year of the gold rush to California. Prices had dropped since then, but they were still high enough that the four strollers passed by.

Andy inquired at the docks about the prospect for passage to San Francisco. He was delighted to learn that two ships, maybe more, were expected from San Francisco any day now.

Two days later, the steamer *Oregon* arrived. A huge throng of Americans crowded the docks. Andy elbowed his way to the front of the mob at the booking office. A collective groan went up from the crowd when an official shouted that the *Oregon* was not returning to San Francisco. It soon became known that the reason the ship was not turning around was that it carried in its hold sacks of gold dust worth $2,000,000. The owners of the hoard would not risk the overland trek across the isthmus. Most passengers decided to remain aboard for the journey around the Horn. It was rumored that many of them also carried large amounts of gold dust in their baggage.

The Americans on the docks were frustrated, some angry, that they were not able to book passage to San Francisco on the *Oregon*, but they were elated to learn that gold in large quantities was still being found in the diggings. Paul, Jason and Stump and Grump stood at the edge of the crowd, listening to all this and waiting for Andy.

Andy remained at the booking office door as the crowd dispersed, some grumbling, others laughing and slapping backs. When all had left, Andy looked around, pulled a flask from his pocket and knocked on the locked door. The door flung open, and a sour-faced clerk stepped into the opening. Holding the flask in front of him, Andy talked with the clerk whose countenance changed from grim to open. He stepped aside, and Andy entered. The door closed.

The four stared at the door in silence, waiting. Then Grump wandered across the wharf to stand at the edge, searching the water below, gently lapping against the stanchions. Jason, Paul and Stump walked to a stone embankment opposite the wharf and sat in the shade of a large lime tree.

An hour passed before the booking office door opened. Andy stood in the doorway, facing inside, apparently still talking. He backed from the door, followed by a smiling, rosy-cheeked agent who clapped Andy on the shoulder. Andy pumped the agent's hand and turned to go. A silly smile on his face, the agent backed into the office, and the door closed.

Andy strode across the wharf to his companions who stood at his approach. Grump hurried over, stopping a few steps short of joining the group.

"Don't enter into any long-term obligations, *amigos,*" said Andy. "We are booked on the *Columbus*, expected at any moment. Well, in a day or two. The agent ain't putting out the word 'cause he's afraid of being mobbed. Cost $210 each. When I complained about the price, he said that steerage last year was over $400. Yeah. You'll understand I had to pay a few extra coins to encourage my new friend to book us on the next ship." Andy sobered. "Sorry, but I'll be asking each of you to share in this unexpected, but most fortunate, additional fee."

Grump stepped up to the group. "Uh, Andy." The group started and looked at Grump. It was the first utterance from Grump since reaching Panama City. They waited.

"I'm paying the extra fee."

"What!" said Andy, Paul and Stump in unison.

"I've been a right nuisance on this trip, but that ain't me. I'm a family man who wants to do right by his family, and I've been missing them something awful and having a hard time living with myself and everybody around me." He wiped his face with a sleeve. "Anyway, I'm paying the fee. I sold my hardware business for a good price, and I've brought a nice chunk of the price with me. I've been scared to death of losing it and got real touchy about everything."

Grump extended a hand to Jason. "Jason, I'm sorry. You've been a better friend than I deserve." Jason grasped the hand and shook. "I'm sorry for . . . everything."

Paul had watched all this, open-mouthed. Now he smiled. "I'll be damned. Welcome to the world . . . uh . . ."

"Benjamin, Benjy." They shook hands and slapped backs all around.

# Chapter 5

The five companions stood at a stern rail of the side-wheeler steamship, SS *Columbus*, staring at Panama City receding in the south as the ship rolled in a quickening breeze. They had heard stories in Panama about the old days when sailing ships bound for California had sometimes been forced to turn back when prevailing winds from the north made progress impossible. The side-wheels of the steamer assured a reliable passage.

The journey from Panama to San Francisco would have been very different had not the United States government decided, even before learning of the discovery of gold, that the new American territory on the Pacific was destined to be a valuable possession. The decision led to the creation of the Pacific Mail Steamship Company to carry mail. The original intent of the company did not include carrying passengers. The gold discovery changed everything.

The ship passed a headland, and Panama City was lost from view. The five continued to stare at the headland, silent, as if looking into the past.

"There she goes, boys," said Paul, turning to face forward, "and here we go."

The others turned to the front, silent, listening to the churning of the steam-driven side-wheels and staring at the wild coast and the occasional small seaside village as the ship moved northward and gradually farther from the coast.

Stump, now Mike, broke the silence. "We never talked about it, but I take it you boys are headin' for the diggings."

"Yep," said Andy, looking up at a gull, gliding, seemingly stationary, ten feet above the deck.

"Do you know where?"

"Yep." He looked back at Mike. "Paul and me got two friends already in the diggings. We were all pards in the Santa Fe trade. We were right there when some people going to Californie last year over the southern route told us about the gold discovery, and our friends was bit bad. They sold all their goods and joined the rush. Paul and me were a little edgy about it and didn't bite. But the letter old Howie sent me from Californie convinced us that we needed to go. How 'bout you?"

"I've got a brother who's working a placer near a place called Grass Valley," said Grump, now Bengy. "I got a letter from him last fall. He says it's got a great future, even if the gold plays out. He's doing pretty good with the gold, but he's already looking around for some land to run cattle on. He says he'll work the placer till he has enough money to get a ranch going. He said there's wild cattle all over California, going back to when it was owned by the Spaniards and the Mexicans. All you gotta do is catch 'em and tame 'em. He thinks the miners would be real happy to have a ready source of beef without having to leave the diggings to hunt for meat. Course, I hadn't heard from my brother since last fall, and that means he wrote that letter nigh on a year ago. No telling what's happened since then."

"Well, your plan makes sense," said Andy. "You're going with him, St— uh, Mike?"

Mike smiled. "Yeah, suits me fine. We're a year into the gold rush, maybe too late for us. I was a pretty good cowboy before me and Benjy got bit by the gold bug. A ranch would suit me fine."

"What about you, Jason?" said Benjy.

Jason was studying the distant coast and hazy mountain range beyond. He turned to face Benjy. "Dunno. Don't want to think about it. I'll tag along with Paul and Andy. Let them make decisions for me. Cattle ranch sounds better to me than grubbing for gold, but I don't think these yahoos are interested in tending cows."

"Nope," Paul said. "We coulda tended cows in Missouri. And we coulda had all the free cows we wanted too. Some Texas cowboys told me that the wild longhorns in north Texas was thick as fleas. All you had to do was catch 'em. Kinda like the Spanish cattle here. Point is, I ain't interested in cows nowhere."

"Me neither," said Andy. "We plan to fill us a big sack of gold and then decide what to do with it."

Jason walked forward, leaned against the rail. He looked up at the deep blue sky, clear but for a wispy cloud layer that hung low above the dark coastal range.

The harbor at San Francisco was clogged with hundreds of ships. Flags of many nations flew from their masts. Sailing ships and steamships, war ships and Chinese junks, all vied for wharf space. Some were forced to anchor in the bay for lack of dock berths.

Some of the vessels that crowded the docks and the bay were no longer ships. They were derelicts, ships that last year had transported a multitude of

'49ers who hardly touched the dock before rushing off to the gold fields. The ships were also loaded with all manner of supplies and foodstuffs and patented gold-mining machines. Most of the cargo was offloaded and sold, except for the patented gold-mining machines that had been invented by men who for the most part had never seen gold in nature.

It was the loss of the crew that led to the death of the ships. Members of the crew who were given leave to see the sights of San Francisco went to the mines instead. Other crewmen who were not granted leave simply left. To try to stem the desertion, captains and owners offered double salary, triple salary, quadruple salary, if the sailor would stay on for the return voyage to New England. There were few takers. The bite of the gold bug was virulent and contagious.

Some abandoned ships became warehouses; others served as prisons. Most were stripped of copper, canvas and cordage and anything else useful and left to rot and sink to the muddy bottom.

The five companions knew little of the stories the rotting hulks could tell. The *Columbus* had docked amidst working ships that busily discharged passengers and cargo and prepared for the return voyage. In many ways, the year 1850 in San Francisco was different from 1849, but ship captains still became jittery as they watched crewmembers walking up the gangway to the dock.

Jason and the others stepped off the gangway to the wharf and dropped their bags. They looked up into the light fog under a heavy overcast that shrouded the wharf and adjacent street and shops. They paced about, stomping and jumping, adjusting to solid footing, losing their sea legs.

Andy shivered. "Damn, it's cold." He opened his pack and pulled out a jacket, struggled into it. He looked around at the passersby. "Everbody's wearing coats! Supposed to be summer." Paul and Mike took coats from their packs and donned them. They were experiencing for the first time the usual San Francisco Bay cold summer fog.

The five looked back at the *Columbus* gangway, suddenly noisy and crowded. The last of *Columbus's* passengers had stepped off the gangway. Now crewmen clogged the gangway, striding, pushing, laughing and shouting, bent under the weight of their bags. Once on the wharf, they disappeared into the throngs of people who hurried about their business, heads down, striding across the street and on sidewalks, vanishing in the fog.

"Sure glad we weren't planning to go anywhere else on that ship," said Andy. "I wager the whole crew almost has skedaddled. I hear the captain offered to raise their pay five times, and only a few took him up on it. He sure won't have enough of this crew to return to Panama. He passed me on deck just before we come off. He said this was the third time his crew had deserted him in San Francisco. In the past, he's had to take on the dregs from the grog shops to put a crew together. Now he's starting to worry again."

"Well, that ain't our problem, is it," Paul said. "Now, speaking of grog shops. Let's find us a quiet corner and see if we can stir up some talk and 'toxication."

"Do we need to find a place to stay?" said Jason.

"That question and solution should turn up during our talking to some locals."

Andy turned to Benjy and Mike who were shouldering their bags. "What about you boys?"

"We still have lots of daylight," said Benjy. "We're going to find somebody who can tell us the best way to get to Grass Valley. Should be a coach running in that direction." He lowered his bag to the deck. "It's been a real . . . uh, education . . . traveling with you fellows. Good luck with whatever you decide to do." He extended his hand to Jason. "Jason, you're a kindred spirit. Best of luck to you."

Jason took the hand and shook. "Good luck at Grass Valley," Jason said. "And to you, Mike." He offered his hand, and Mike shook it.

Handshakes and pats on the back, and good lucks and be carefuls, and Mike and Benjy hefted their packs and walked off the wharf. They were soon lost in the pedestrian current in the street and enveloped by the fog.

"Well, there they go," said Andy. "Strange fellows that turned out to be pretty ordinary, after all. Just took a little time and patience." He reached for his pack. "Now, about that grog and conversation." They shouldered their packs and walked off the wharf and across the street toward the Gold Dust Bar and Café, dodging pedestrians anxious to be some other place.

"My best advice for you boys is to get on the first ship leaving San Francisco, one that'll take you back to the good 'ol U.S. of A."

The three companions sat at a corner table of the smoky bar with two men, strangers only at the first glass. The men were dressed in plain, clean work clothes. Recent shaves revealed nicks and chafing, evidence that a clear face was not their usual condition.

"We've seen the elephant, and it stomped hell out of us. We've got just about enough left in our poke to get home. You said you come in on the *Columbus?* Thanks for bringin' it in. We're leavin' on it. Already talked with the captain. He said he's leaving soon as he can get a crew together. Most of his crew is heading for the diggings.

"Hell, we're gonna crew ourselves! He said he's paying five times the usual. Our pay will get us to Panama, and we'll see what happens then. Right, Dicken?" He turned to his companion. Dicken nodded, staring into his glass.

Dicken looked up. "If you fellas are determined to give it a shot, I'd head for the southern mines, if I was you. I've heard they're still producing. We was in the north, all around Grass Valley, and the placers seem to be about played out. At least, wherever we worked."

Jason, Paul and Andy exchanged grim glances.

"We talked with a couple of fellas yesterday who showed us a sack of dust that was most impressive," said Dicken. "They said they took it in just a week at a placer they worked in the south. They left two partners there to guard the place while they come to San Francisco to buy some tools and goods and bullets and raise some hell. They been in the mountains almost six months and hadn't seen a glass of whiskey in all that time. Nor 'uh woman." He smiled.

"You can also get to the southern diggings faster than the north. Here's what those two old boys said. You go down to the wharf . . ."

*****

Andy and Paul stood at the rail amidships of the small stern-wheel steamboat, *Captain Sutter,* churning up the San Joaquin River, bound for Stockton. Deciding not to rely completely on the two lapsed miners who told them the best way to get to the southern mines, they had consulted the bartender who confirmed their advice. He had referred them to the agent on the wharf who happily booked them for an early morning departure the following day. The three had accepted with thanks the agent's invitation to sleep that night on the ship's deck.

At daybreak, bright sunshine flooded the ship and land and burned off the fog. Jason stood at the stern, watching the huge wheel churning slowly, water dripping from the horizontal paddles. The sky was clear, and large expanses of clear water on the valley floor sparkled. Rafts of ducks and other waterfowl burst into flight at the passage of the noisy ship.

Paul and Andy walked up behind Jason and leaned on the rail. "Jason, we got to parley," said Paul. Jason turned to face them, his face blank.

"We're planning to buy what we need in Stockton and pack it to the diggings. I'm told that we shouldn't have any problem finding our friends—that's Gus and Howie—since miners talk a lot with each other and move around a lot. We'll find somebody who knows them. I'm real glad the two yahoos in the Gold Dust Bar and Café confirmed that the southern mines is the place to be since that's where we was going anyhow.

"We plan to work with Gus and Howie and learn the trade. But we think before long, we'll go off on our own. I hope you'll go with us from Stockton to our friends' claim. And you'll be most welcome to come with us if we decide to split."

"You're good friends," said Jason. "I appreciate the offer. I'll pay my share for the goods." Andy and Paul waited, but he said no more. He nodded and walked to the other side of the boat, stared at the bank and the flooded fields and sloughs.

Andy and Paul watched. Andy frowned. "That boy's got to pull out of this someday. I feel for him, but his mood is getting to me. Man, I want to be upbeat about what we got coming up, but he makes it hard."

"Yeah, know what you mean," Paul said.

Jason looked up at the smoke that billowed from the top of the single stack and lined out horizontally over the stern from the motion of the boat and a light headwind. He faced forward, closed his eyes, felt the cooling breeze on his face. He opened his eyes in time to see a dozen wild turkeys foraging at the edge of a thicket of willow scrub on the bank. Farther on, two does leaped from a stand of cottonwood at the approach of the boat. They ran along the bank, stopped, looked at the steamer. They bolted suddenly, stopped and looked again, remaining frozen as the boat passed.

"Pretty, ain't they?"

Jason turned to see a crewman standing at the rail. "Yes, they are."

"I make this run reg'lar', and I never get tired of it. Don't see much like this back home. I'm from New York, myself. Been here almost a year now. Came out for the gold, like most everbody else around here. I got tired of that business real fast." He smiled, still looking at the land.

"Can't beat this," the crewman said. Suddenly he straightened, leaned over the rail. "Look at that! Right there!" He pointed toward a large animal at the edge of a pond, alerted, looking nervously around.

"I see it. Is that an elk?" said Jason. "I heard about them."

"Yeah, but that's not what I'm pointing at. Look off to the right of the elk, beside that clump of willows. See that brown spot in front of the green brush?"

Jason searched, then: "I see it. Is that . . . is that a . . . *bear?"*

"Yeah! That's it. That's a grizzly, and he's eyeing that elk!"

The elk caught the bear's scent or saw movement, and it bounded away. The grizzly thrust its nose in the air, waved his head side-to-side, then circled back and retreated slowly.

"Man! That was a big 'un. Don't see many grizzlies 'round here now," said the crewman. "Lots more last year when I first come. Hunters been taking 'em reg'larly since then. With all the people coming in, won't be long before they'll be gone from the valley. Still lots in the mountains, I'm told."

Jason stared at the expanse, now seemingly empty of birds and animals. The crewman walked away toward the bow.

*Jessie and the kids would love this. Glimpses of the wild without the hardship of living in the wild. Why must we always punish ourselves, choosing to do things and go places when we are not unhappy with our present condition? Both of our families have been moving for generations. Jessie said it. We weren't unhappy. We had a good farm and good friends. The children had a good school and liked their teacher. The land in western Kentucky could be harsh, but it could also be beautiful, soft and rewarding. Why did we leave? Are dreams of the unknown better than the reality we know and love? It's all my fault. My fault.*

He moved quickly to the side of the cabin and collapsed on a bench facing the shore, sobbing, his hands covering his face as he rocked, back and forth, back and forth.

The great central valley, the Stockton merchant called it. The flat land stretched for miles eastward to a high mountain range that ran north and south as far as they could see. The Sierra Nevada, the merchant said. Tall peaks wearing a mantle of white-gray snow rose from the range, seeming to pierce the sky. Below this, a belt of dark purple describing dense forests and lower still, foothills of a lighter hue of green and tan.

The three mounted partners were led by Will, the packer. Everyone had agreed that they wanted to reach the diggings as soon as possible, and the cost of renting saddle horses and two pack mules would quickly be recovered in their getting to work as early as possible. Or so they told themselves.

They rode through a riot of color. Carpets of brilliant orange poppies and blue lupine, light pink cat's ears, purple owl's clover and foothill penstemon. Jason pulled his mount up and let the others move ahead. He wiped his eyes with a sleeve.

They camped that night in a field of poppies so dense that Jason winced at having to lay his bedroll on the orange carpet.

Leaving the flat valley behind at first light, Will led the procession into the foothills, following well-trod trails through scattered oaks and pines and cedars.

The riders pulled slickers from packs when a light rain began falling. The cloud passed, and the sprinkle was replaced with bright sunshine. They removed the slickers and tied them behind saddles.

As the ascent steepened, the solitary trail soon branched to narrow paths that ran off into forests and canyons carpeted with blooming manzanita, ferns, wildflowers and scattered shrubs.

Now riders occasionally were seen on the main trail and crisscross branches. Andy and the packer waved and hallooed and stopped riders to ask about Andy's friends, Howie and Gus. Some riders stopped and listened, shook their heads and rode on; a few simply ignored Andy and continued on their way.

Finally, a grizzled old-timer listened with interest, replied enthusiastically with an abundance of arm waving, and pointed down a feeder path. Andy thanked him, and he and Will rode back to Paul and Jason.

"Well, we got a good lead. Will here thinks he knows where Gus and Howie are working." The packer led off and reined his horse off the main trail onto a feeder path. After an hour on this trail, they turned off on yet another branch and followed this path through a thick stand of pines.

The trail opened abruptly at the bank of a stream of clear water, about ten feet wide with a gentle flow. They rode upstream on the bank and around a turning at a willow thicket.

They pulled up at a rough camp. "Gus! Howie!" shouted Andy.

Immediately, a man appeared from behind the tent. "Andy! That you? That you, Paul?" He grinned. "Be damned! It is!" He strode down the bank to the riders.

The four riders dismounted. Andy and Gus shook hands and clapped each other on the shoulders. Paul and Gus shook and resisted the impulse to embrace.

A figure emerged from the woods behind a tent. "By god, I thought I heard the screethins' of old comrades, and sure enough I did!" He almost ran down the bank.

"Howie!" shouted Paul. Andy and Paul grabbed him by two hands, and they shook and clapped shoulders and squeezed arms.

Jason and the packer stood where they had dismounted, holding the reins of horses and mules.

"Gus, Howie, this is Jason. Jason come with us all the way from Independence just to meet you fine fellows." He grinned. "Well, not just to meet you. He decided to join us when I told him we were going to fill up our sacks with gold and go home rich men." Gus and Paul advanced and pumped Jason's hand.

"Well, I hope these two old reprobates hadn't corrupted you too far," said Gus. "If they have, we'll have to set you straight. As for filling your bags with dust and goin' home rich, we need to talk." He laughed out loud.

"This is Will," said Jason, gesturing to the packer. "He delivered us here in good shape." Hand shakes all around.

"If you gents are all settled," said Will, "I'll take my pay and be off." While the old friends were getting reacquainted, he had unloaded his mules, leaving the packs in a tidy pile.

"Right you are," said Andy. He rummaged in his pack, pulled out a small leather bag, extracted a handful of coins and counted the fee into Will's hand.

The packer raised a hand to his forehead in thanks. "Soon's you fellows want to haul out your gold, I'll be ready. Just send word to Stockton, and I'll see if I can round up enough mules to carry the load."

Andy and Paul laughed. Gus looked solemnly at Howie. They watched Will mount and lead his animals to the trail.

Gus turned back to the others. "Okay, here's what's goin' down. It looks like it could sprinkle, so you need to get your tent set up. You did bring some canvas?"

"Yep," said Andy.

"Gus, fix us a bite," said Howie, "and then we'll talk about Santa Fe and what we're missing. And then we'll show you what it is we do here."

The three newcomers pulled their packs to a level spot behind Gus and Paul's tent and set about unpacking.

Gus and Howie had chosen their placer as much for its beauty as its promise. The site was shaded by huge black oaks and Ponderosa pines. The bank from the fire pit to the stream was open and sandy, free of any shrubbery. About fifteen feet wide and shallow at this point, the stream flowed placidly before their camp, then dropped down a slope where the banks were clogged with a tangled undergrowth beneath large oak trees.

The five men sat on short lengths of logs around a fire pit set in a circle of stones. The fire had died to embers, still glowing and sending up a thin spiral of gray smoke that rose and disappeared in the faint breeze. Empty tin plates lay on the ground at their feet.

"That was one fine meal," said Paul. "Best venison I ever eat."

"Glad you liked it. You'll have more for dinner, and breakfast and every meal til the carcass is clean," Howie said. "We're pretty short on fruits and vegetables, and that's not good. Couple of fellas a few miles north got the scurvy, I'm told, and the doc said it was because they had been living on meat and no fruits and vegetables. Maybe one of you boys will put in a garden 'stead of grubbing for gold." He smiled, looked around. "Yeah, I know, not likely."

The group fell silent as Gus and Howie and Andy pulled out pipes. They filled and lit the pipes, rested against the logs and puffed, sending spirals of smoke overhead.

"Have you always worked this spot?" said Andy. "Or do you move around?"

Gus puffed, lowered his pipe, blew out smoke. "We've camped at this spot since we got here. Suits us fine. Course, we've also done what every other miner has done, gone off following some tom fool story about somebody making a big strike. When the word gits out that somebody's hit a rich spot, everbody in hearing rushes off, digs and pans and thrashes around till they're convinced that it's a bust, then they go back to their own camp. We've done a bit of that, but give it up as a waste of time."

"Do you ever get tired of your own company?" said Paul.

Howie looked at Gus. "Now that's a good question. Mining the streams is a lonely business, and some people cain't handle it. Gus and me have been pards for a long time, goin' back to Santa Fe. We take each other for granted now, git along real fine.

"That don't apply to everbody out here. I heard a story a while back that up north they found a corpse at a rough camp, and the old boy was holding a note in his fist that said 'Deserted by my friends but not by God.'"

"Yeah," Gus said. "They say he starved to death. Too bad God didn't give the old boy something to eat."

Howie glanced sideways at Gus, grim-faced. "Don't git off on that."

The group fell silent, puffing on their pipes and staring into the fire. Howie looked over at Paul. "I 'member you had a sweet spot for pretty little Carmen at the *Tres Piños* cantina, Paul," said Howie, grinning. "You shoulda brought her with you. We miss female companionship here. We went to Stockton a couple of times for supplies and groceries, but they're short on women too.

"We don't need to go that far now, for groceries, I mean. Fella from San Francisco gave up on panning and set up a store in a big tent just a few miles north. He sells groceries and some clothes. He said he's going to add mining supplies. Real convenient. Get our mail there too. Some other people have begun to move in there as well. They got a livery and a blacksmith shop. He thinks there will be a town soon. We're getting real civilized. There's a couple of board buildings going up right now."

"Back to the original subject," Gus said. "Only woman around here is a Indian woman just up around the bend. She's up there with a couple fellas. She sure don't like the arrangement. They seem to be pretty hard on her. We hear things. Saw her a couple of times across the stream. She didn't look happy. We thought about taking a hand in it, but the rule in the diggings is to mind your own business."

"Speakin' of business," said Howie, "let's show you around. Good thing you arrived here on a Sunday. Sunday's a rest day. Most of the miners take a day off and wash dishes and clothes and relax. I even got a book I'm reading." He stood. "Lemme show you what we did last season and what every miner begins with." He walked to a brush lean-to beside the tent and picked up a pan. "C'mon, I'll show you."

Paul, Andy and Jason stood and followed Howie to the stream. He showed them the pan he carried. The pan was stamped iron, flat-bottomed with sloping sides, about three inches deep and eighteen inches wide.

"This looks like a plain old wash pan, but it's the most useful tool in camp. This is what every miner begins with."

Howie knelt at the water's edge, dipped the pan in the shallows and scooped up a wedge of loose sand and gravel and about a quarter pan of water. He combed through the soil with his fingers, tossed out pebbles and bark and the like. He then submerged the pan and rocked it in a circular motion, which swirled the water around, washing out the debris and sand. Soon there was only a small bit of sand in the bottom. He lifted the pan, pushed the sand around and around with his fingers—and held the pan out to show the others a single gold flake in the bottom.

"Well, I'll be a monkey's uncle. Look at that." said Andy, peering into the pan. "So that's the way it's done. Looks easy."

"Yeah," said Howie. "Easy. Just whirl it around, and the gold goes to the bottom, being heavier than all the other stuff." He picked up the gold flake and handed the pan to Andy. "Give it a try."

Andy took the pan, smiled. He knelt and imitated Howie. After ten minutes of removing gravel, swirling the pan, pushing the sand around the bottom with a hand, tilting the pan, swirling again, he stood, straightened, rubbed the small of the back with his free hand.

"Nothing," Andy said.

"It's all right," said Howie, "happens all the time. Now do this maneuver fifty times before going to bed tonight. That's the way to pan for gold." Andy grimaced. Howie smiled, slapped Andy on the back. "You'll get the hang of it." Howie laughed.

"Actually, we don't use the pan much any more," said Gus. "Come up here." He walked toward a contraption that sat back from the bank. The others followed.

"This here's a rocker. Some people call it a cradle." He explained how it worked, pointing to the parts of the cradle and demonstrating how each functioned.

The device was a wooden box with a channel about four feet long and two feet wide. It was shaped like a cradle, mounted on semicircular pieces of wood to facilitate rocking. Soil was dumped into a box, or hopper, at the upper end. Then water was poured over the soil, which was then washed down the sloping channel. Handles attached to the rocker were moved back and forth to agitate the soil as the water flowed over it. Narrow wooden riffles that stretched across the bottom of the channel caught the heavier gold while the lighter material flowed out over the riffles, dumping at the lower end of the channel, which was open.

"It's not as good as the pan," said Howie, "but we can work a helluva lot more soil, and it's a helluva lot easier on the back. Sometimes we catch the debris that comes out at the bottom and work it with the pan to get any flakes that flowed over the riffles."

"I'm for the rocker," said Andy.

"Actually, there's something else called a tom that makes the job even easier. It works pretty much like the rocker and handles a lot more soil, but it's bigger and needs a steady source of water to flow over it. I saw one the other day 'bout a half mile upstream. Looks interesting, but it's beyond us now. Maybe with you three in the camp now, we can think on it. It would mean building some waterworks. We'll see."

"There's one more thing I want to show you before we get back to our Sunday siesta," said Gus. He motioned for the others to follow. They walked behind him to a small shack of weathered boards set in a thicket behind their tent. A neatly dressed carcass of a young buck with a small rack hung from a limb beside the shack. The shack and deer were not visible from the stream bank.

Gus stopped at the front of the shack, pushed the door open. There at the back of the dark interior sat a black cast iron cook stove. The legs rested on a metal plate and had a corrugated pipe chimney that reached up to a hole in the sloping roof. Gus beamed.

"Well, I'll be damned," said Andy. "Where in hell did you get that thing?"

Gus grinned from ear to ear. "Fella brought it up last fall, said he planned to open a café, but got bit by the gold bug, and off he went. He was just going to leave it, but I gave him $5.00 anyway."

"Does it work?" said Paul.

"Hell, yes, it works! I'll prove it! Howie, how 'bout roasting up some deer meat this evening, and I'll add something from the cook shack!"

"I can do that," said Howie. He looked around. "You boys mind having deer meat again for dinner?"

"If it's as good as what we already had, oh, yeah," said Andy.

The newcomers looked around the shack. Shelves on two walls were sparsely stocked with canned food and cooking oil and pots and pans.

"Where do you get all this stuff?" said Andy. I hadn't seen no store this side of Stockton. "

"Well, you said it," Howie said. "Fella from Stockton every now and then comes in his wagon loaded with supplies. He visits the camps until he's sold out. We don't buy much from him. He's expensive. We try to rely on hunting and fishing as much as we can. Some necessary things you can't do without, though, like oysters and a little rum." He smiled.

Howie explained why they bought little from the Stockton merchant. Flour cost two dollars a pound, sugar and coffee, four dollars, eggs a dollar each. His New England rum, transported in a barrel, was twenty dollars for a quart, and the buyer had to provide his own container.

"Them prices ain't too bad if you're bringing in ten ounces of gold a day," said Howie, "but we don't ordinarily take that much, so we eat a lot of deer and squirrel." He collected a butcher knife and large fork from a shelf and walked toward the door. "Okay, now for that deer meat."

# Chapter 6

Jason walked slowly upstream along the edge of the placid flow, head down, hands in pockets. He had left the others in camp, doing what Gus said miners do on a Sunday. Howie washed clothes at streamside, draping the wet things on low bushes. Gus sat on the ground at camp, leaning against the trunk of a large oak, reading a borrowed book, the cover and pages soiled from being held by hands that worked outside. Paul napped in the tent while Andy, sitting on a log out front, cleaned his rifle.

Approaching a streamside willow thicket, Jason stopped at a series of sharp chirps, looked up into the treetops across the stream, searched for the singer. The bird took flight, displaying its blue wings and head and orange flashes on the breast. He watched until the bird disappeared over the canopy. He had seen his first western bluebird.

He resumed his stroll, came up to the thicket. And saw her. She stood knee-deep in the shallows, rock-still, staring at him. Water dripped from her wet hair and ran in rivulets down her naked brown body, thin streams snaking down her flat belly to her thighs.

Her round face was soft, pretty. Her eyes were opened wide, her lips slightly parted, revealing perfect white teeth. She was frozen, tense, poised to take flight. He saw the cut on her cheek.

He was mesmerized. Should he say something, or retreat, or . . . what? Then he heard a faint shout. She turned her head abruptly upstream. She waded quickly from the water and disappeared behind the thicket, but not before he saw the dark welts on her back and buttock.

He closed his eyes, shook his head vigorously, rubbed his face with both hands. He stared at the stream where she had stood, then turned and walked slowly back to camp.

In the days that followed, Jason took his turns at the rocker, at first learning, now enduring, the monotonous rhythm: dumping soil into the hopper, dousing with water, moving the rocker back and forth with the handle, running his fingers through the wet soil in the channel, extracting the occasional flakes, wondering whether he could endure another day of the mindless chore.

He preferred the solitary panning. Squatting at the edge of the stream, or even stooping in the shallows, he swirled the silt in the pan, setting up little whirlpools, raking the silt with his fingers, whirling the pan again, draining the debris into the water, picking up the golden flakes and dropping them into the jar on the bank.

Staring into the swirling sand, his mind raced. He saw the Kentucky farm, Jessie at the kitchen stove, humming a gospel song, Christian rubbing down his pony, Nicole swaying slowly in the swing hanging by thin ropes from an oak limb, her hair wild, eyes closed, smiling. The images faded, replaced by a young brown woman standing in the shallows, water streaming down her naked body, her face a mask.

"Jason, you been on that pan a spell. You trying to turn that sand to gold?" Jason looked up at a smiling Andy.

Jason stood, flexed his back. “Lose track of time sometimes.” He handed Andy the pan, walked to the rocker and took over from Paul, who clapped him on the shoulder and walked away, swinging his arms to restore circulation.

After dumping soil into the hopper, Jason poured water on the heap, rocked the cradle with the handle, staring into space.

Andy watched him, shook his head. He squatted at the streamside, dipped the pan in the water.

Jason was about to pour another load of soil into the hopper when he stopped abruptly and looked toward the willow thicket. He heard it again, the faint cry of the Indian woman, then the angry shout of a man. A moment later, she cried out again, followed by a distant, muffled cursing tirade.

He set the bucket on the ground, still looking at the thicket.

“Don’t get involved,” said Gus. He had walked up when Jason had been concentrating on the rocker.

Jason glanced at him, then back at the thicket. Another anguished cry, softer this time.

He strode toward the thicket.

“Jason, don’t do it,” called Gus.

Another cry. As Jason came abreast of the thicket, he heard sobbing. He walked through a narrow cut in the thicket, pushing boughs away as he passed. Emerging from the passage, he stopped. He saw the camp about thirty yards upstream. One man squatted at the stream edge, holding a pan, motionless, watching him. The miner stood, picked up a small bag at his feet and set it higher on the bank.

The other man’s back was to him. He stood before the tent, bending over the Indian woman that he held tightly by an arm. He spoke in low tones that Jason could not make out. She raised an arm before her face and turned away. He raised a quirt of braided leather straps that Jason had not seen until that moment. He pulled her around and struck her on the back. She cried out.

Jason broke into a run. By the time he reached the camp, the man at the bank had stood and said something to his partner. When Jason came up to the girl's tormentor, the man turned to face him, still holding her tightly by an arm. She whimpered, wiped her face with the back of a hand.

"This ain't none of your affair, mister. Get off my claim."

Jason stood his ground. "Let her go," he said softly.

"I said this ain't none of your affair." His face hardened, and he raised the quirt, threatening Jason.

Jason punched him hard in the stomach. The man bent forward, gasping, released the girl. Jason reached over and pulled the quirt from his hand. "Now, you son of a bitch, you're going to see what this feels like." Jason raised the quirt.

"Hold it right there, friend." The miner at the streamside held a pistol leveled at Jason. "What do we do about this busybody, Fred? Do we solve this problem before it becomes a problem?" The pistol still pointed at Jason.

Fred inhaled deeply, straightened. He stepped over slowly to Jason, took the quirt from his hand. "We could do that. Yes, we could. But his pards might wonder what happened to him when they see his body floating by."

He leaned into Jason's face. Jason turned aside at the heavy alcoholic stench. The man grasped Jason's chin and jerked his head back to face him. He spoke softly. "This is my camp. Keep outta my camp." He motioned with his head toward the Indian woman. "That there's *my* woman. She ain't no concern of yours. Are you understanding all this?"

Jason did not blink, remained rigid. The man leaned back, raised the quirt and swung it, striking Jason's cheek as he turned away. Blood bubbled from the cut.

"Now get outta my camp."

Jason glanced over the man's shoulder at the woman. She cowered behind him, both hands at her face, her eyes brimming with tears over cheeks already marked with dry tear tracks.

He turned and walked toward the thicket.

Jason sat on a log beside his tent, a canvas bag at his feet. He held a small leather pouch, hefted it. Each Sunday morning, Gus divided the week's gold take among the five partners. The average daily take was about an ounce and a half each, a respectable figure, said Gus. Jason had watched his accumulation grow week by week, without taking any particular satisfaction in it.

Dropping the pouch into the bag, he pulled out the Colt Dragoon. He poured powder into five cylinders and pushed a ball inside each, tamped the balls down. He spun the cylinder slowly until the pin rested on the empty chamber.

He stared at the pistol, turning it over in his hands. What am I doing? I didn't want to buy a pistol because it had only one use, to shoot people. Is this something I want to do? If I see the son of a bitch hit the girl again, yeah, it's something I want to do.

"Jason, you're about to buy yourself a passel of trouble." Jason looked up to see Andy. "I see he nicked you." Jason put a hand to the cut on his cheek.

Jason pushed the pistol into the sack, looked up at Andy. "You said you didn't cotton to slavery, a man owning a human being like he owns an animal. That son of a bitch is treating her like a slave."

"That's true, I did say that, and I believe that. She probably is a slave, Jason. Gus and I talked about it when you went over there. Seems owning Indians in California has been common for years, many years, since California was Spanish. Seems there's some opposition to the practice now, but it's still common."

"That doesn't make it right." Jason lowered his head, shook it slowly. "God, I hate to see anybody abused by somebody who thinks he has a right."

"I understand. But you're not in Kentucky or Missouri now, son. You're in the California gold country where the law lays its hands on lightly, and people have to get along on their own. Just keep in mind that whatever you do is going to have an effect on everybody in this camp."

Jason pulled the sack between his feet. "Thanks, Andy. I'll remember."

Andy smiled, nodded, turned to leave.

"Andy." He turned back. "I never really thanked you and Paul for taking me in. I'm sorry I have been so down, so negative, when you want to think of all this in a really positive light. I'll never forget your kindness."

Andy frowned. "I don't like where this is headed."

Jason leaned back, smiled. "Never mind. Just sounding off. Doesn't mean a thing." He looked down at the sack, pulled the drawstring. He stood, holding the sack.

"Andy. I don't know how to put this, but if you ever find me gone, know that it's because I have decided to move on, and there was some good reason to leave. I would never just disappear. I would let you know what's happening. Just don't think bad of me."

"Stop it! We could never think bad of you, son." Andy clapped him on a shoulder. "And stop talking like a damn fool. You ain't going nowhere. Hear?"

Gus and Howie, working the rocker, had listened to the talk, now walked over. They rubbed wet hands on their trousers. Jason nodded to them.

Jason smiled. "One other thing," he said. "You might have noticed that I have a particular fondness for this coat that I either wear or have near all the time."

Gus and Howie looked at each other. "No, I hadn't noticed," said Gus. "So you're wearing a coat. It's gettin' cold."

"I noticed," said Paul. "You wore it in Panama when it was too hot even for clothes, or you had it strapped to your pack."

"Let me show you why. Feel this." He held the bottom of the coat out. Paul felt it.

He frowned. "Be damned. What is it?"

"Feel the collar," said Jason.

Paul and Gus touched the collar, felt something hard and felt along the collar.

"Be damned!" said Gus. "It's filled! What is it?"

"Gold pieces, mostly $10 eagles, some half eagles. Jessie's idea. She was afraid of getting robbed. She sewed these in at the farm before we left. I take out a coin when I need it and stitch it back up."

"Pretty smart, your Jessie. Uh, sorry."

"Yeah." Jason looked aside. "Well, I'm telling you this now, in case . . . in case—"

"In case nothing!" Andy said. "You ain't going nowhere, and nothing's gonna happen to you. Understand?"

Jason smiled, walked to the tent opening, ducked his head and went through. Inside, he set the bag beside his pack. He checked the rifle, confirmed that it was loaded and leaned it against the pack. He had bought the lightly-used rifle in San Francisco, assuming that he would need to hunt for the pot, no matter where he went from there. It was a caplock Leman, nothing like the Hawken he lost in the fire, but it was cheaper and in good condition. It should suffice.

He had become accustomed of late in accepting substitutes for things once treasured.

The days passed in regular order. Breakfast at first light, panning at streamside, working the rocker, a short break for a lunch of sorts, panning and rocking, supper at the campfire, passing around a bottle, stories of Santa Fe and cantinas and sloe-eyed, smiling *señoritas*. More than once, Jason noticed a hard-bitten miner turn aside and wipe a tear.

Some miners, anxious to fill their gold sacks, worked seven days a week, but most took Sunday off from their labors. Jason and his partners followed this custom, not from any religious impulse, but from habits they had formed in previous lives. They washed clothes, read books and aged newspapers that were passed from camp to camp. Sitting around the fire pit at midday, they exchanged stories and lies, laughing softly and slapping backs.

Occasionally on a Sunday, they wandered to emerging settlements nearby to watch horse races or foot races, or a dogfight. Or sampling the offerings at a new saloon, successfully avoiding risking their dust at the faro and monte tables. They also passed by the improvised church services overseen by a zealous layman or itinerant preacher.

At work and at rest, Jason had tried to ignore the faint sounds coming from the placer upstream, but he knew what was happening, and it gnawed on him. He stood often at the thicket that separated the two camps, his head down, listening to the angry shouts and anguished, soft cries of the woman.

At supper, as they sat around the fire circle, he listened to the repeated admonitions of the others. Don't get involved; it's none of our affair. He listened and said nothing.

Popular topics at the evening fires were the tales that were passed along among the camps. True tales, tall tales, lies and questionable news. One evening, Gus told a story he had heard just a week before the arrival of his Santa Fe amigos and Jason.

It seems a miner a few miles north had a run of bad luck. He had been taking about an ounce a day for some time, then his take dried up. One day after panning for hours at streamside and taking nothing, not a single flake, he told his wife he was going to try his luck a mile or so upstream. While he was away, his little girl went to the spot where he had been panning and waded in the shallows. She stepped on something hard, raked the sand with her fingers and picked it up. It was a stone of some sort covered with a sticky mess. She took it to her mother who cleaned off the mess. What was left was a lump of pure gold, weighing about six or seven pounds. When the word got out, every miner within five miles came to the camp and worked every inch of the stream on both sides and found nothing. Not a flake.

"True story. I was one of the miners who worked that spot for most of a day while the man and his wife sat in the shade, watching us. I asked the fella if I could see the nugget, but he wasn't obliging. The little girl couldn't stop smiling."

"Happens all the time," said Howie. "Down south of here couple of months ago, word got out that a huge pocket of gold had been discovered on a feeder creek, and every miner in the district rushed over the hill to the spot, loaded up with crowbars, pickaxes, spades, rifles and pans.

"At the end of the day, they all returned to their camps, bone tired and hungry, with empty pockets, but laughing and joking. Most of these boys grumble and complain, but they're a good lot, most of 'em."

The five sat quiet, staring into the flames, drawing on pipes, looking up at the darkening sky. Gus tossed a few short sticks into the fire that ignited quickly in the hot embers.

"Yep, gold is where you find it," said Gus.

The others waited, staring at Gus.

"Well, tell it, dammit," said Andy.

"Okay, since you ask so politely. I was walking upstream one Sunday, just taking a break, when I saw this old gray-haired man, sitting on a rock at streamside, his pan at his feet. He was dressed in old clothes that just hung on him. He was beat, staring at the ground. I asked him what was wrong. He said he had been working this spot for days and hadn't even an ounce of gold to show for it. I looked around the site, checking it out, you see. I told him to look under the rock he was sitting on.

"He sorta looked at me, frowned, but said he would do it to please me. We pushed the rock over and saw a bunch of moss. He pulled the moss away and saw a couple of crevices in the rock. He reached in the crevices and pulled out a bunch of little gold nuggets that looked like pumpkin seeds. His eyes got so big I thought they would jump out of his head. When he finished, I figure the lot would weigh over half a pound.

"True story." The others arched eyebrows and smiled.

"Did you hear about the discovery a few miles north of here?" Howie said. "A newcomer in his first day in the country found a solid chunk of gold that weighed out at twenty-three pounds. Perfect cube, like somebody had poured it into a mold."

Andy stood, knocked out his pipe on a stone at the fire circle. "I'll git to my bed on that one."

The days and weeks passed, one day much like the one that preceded it. Jason worked hard, taking his share of gold flakes at the stream and the rocker. He worked from dawn to dusk, his mind sometimes a void, other times filled with dark memories, regrets and longing. Sometimes he worked so late one of the partners had to tell him to stop and join them at supper.

On one particular evening, after a long workday, the five partners sat on logs or on the ground, their backs against logs. Empty tin plates lay on the ground. They stared into the fire pit, embers glowing red and yellow and orange, tiny flames erupting and quickly vanishing, shedding scant light at sundown.

A light breeze fanned the embers, sending up a spiral of sparks. A large red leaf drifted in the light breeze over the fire to the ground, then another and another. They looked up into the canopy.

Busy with their labors, they had hardly noticed the approach of autumn. Now the forest displayed an explosive array of color, the golden leaves of the black oak, prized by the Indians for its abundant supply of acorns, the dogwood's red leaves and the large yellow leaves of the big leaf maple. Dark green Ponderosa pines contrasted with the bright hues of the deciduous forest.

Paul tossed some sticks into the fire. The dry sticks burst into flame. "Soon as you've filled your sack with nuggets and dust, what do you plan to do, boys?" he said.

"I'll tell you what I'm gonna do," Howie said. "I'm going back to Missouri, buy me a first-rate wagon and team and load it with goods and head for Santa Fe. I've missed it. What with it being a U. S. of A. territory now, it's bound to take off."

"I know what you miss, old friend," said Gus. "You miss the *señoritas*, that's what?" He grinned.

Howie looked over at Gus, wrinkled his forehead, smiled thinly. "Well, there's that."

"I'm with you, old man," said Gus. "I miss the trade and Santa Fe, too." He looked across the fire at Paul and Andy and Jason. "How 'bout you boys?"

"Hadn't thought much about it," said Andy. "Santa Fe still sounds good to me, but the trail doesn't. Think I might settle around Santa Fe. Maybe drive some cows from Missouri and set up a ranch. Growing population 'round there should mean a good market for beef." He looked at Paul.

"Damn if I know," Paul said. "Maybe I'll wait to see what you boys set up and join the best prospect." He smiled, slapped Andy on the knee.

"How 'bout you, Jason?" said Gus. All looked at Jason, waited.

Jason stirred the embers with a stick. "Dunno." He looked up. "Maybe I'll take root right here."

"Not unless you grow fur or fins," said Gus. "Winter here is pretty fierce and unpredictable. If it's mild with lots of rain, there's too much water for panning. If it's colder with lots of snow, there's no runoff, and streams might freeze solid. Either way, winter is hard on miners. Last winter, most miners 'round here packed up and went down to the valley. Howie and me went to Stockton. With the beginnings of a town up the way here, some might think this winter of setting up there. I haven't decided what we should do.

"There may be another reason to head down the hill soon. We might be settin' in a war zone. There's been Indian problems off and on, but there're beginning to heat up. I talked with some boys from down south at the store yesterday." He looked at Jason. "News moves fast up and down the diggings.

"Indian problems go back a long way. I'm told when gold was first discovered, some Indians prospected on their own, and some were hired by white miners. It wasn't long before all Indians were chased from the placers, and that didn't set well with them.

"Other Indians were mad at the whites for invading their lands. They saw their acorn oaks bein' cut down and the game killed or chased away by the whites. So they began to fight back. They raided miners' camps, stole from them, and generally made nuisances of theirselves. Even killed some miners.

"It's got so bad down south lately that there's talk of a military campaign against the Indians to force them to move to reservations in the valley. The Indians heard this talk, and it just made 'em madder. We're lucky we haven't seen any of that, but I'm told the problem will spread all over the gold country. So you see why staying here over the winter might not be too healthy.

"Seems a man named Savage down south at Mariposa is behind the talk of a military operation. Word is that he doesn't want a war; he just wants to persuade the Indians that they must go to the reservation in the valley or be killed off. He thinks they'll be reasonable once they understand the options.

"Savage has done a lot of business with the Indians for years and thinks he has good relations with them. Hell, he has five Indian wives who keep him informed about what their kin are doing."

"Sounds pretty serious," said Andy. "With five wives, he don't need to go outside his own house to find trouble." He guffawed.

"Yeah, you might be right," said Gus. "Anyway. One of the fellas I talked with said he was going to Mariposa to join the expedition that Savage is putting together. He asked me if I wanted to join as well."

"Seems to me the Indians have a right to protect their lands from outsiders," said Jason.

"Hmm," this from Gus.

"Have any Indians done any mining around here, or worked for miners?" said Jason.

"Not since we been here," said Gus. "We've not really had any contact with Indians."

"Except those three last summer," said Howie.

"Oh, yeah," said Gus. "That was strange. Interesting, though. We was panning right here when these three Indians walked out of the trees across the stream. They just stood on the bank there with their long bows, looking at us. We didn't know what to think. Then they waded across, held up hands in greeting like. One said something in his language. Course we didn't understand a word.

"He pointed at a red cloth belt that I had hung on a limb after washing it, then pointed to his chest. I took it that he wanted the belt. Hell, I wasn't about to give it to him, but he took out a gold nugget from a little bag tied at his waist. The other two Indians also showed nuggets, almost as big as the first one. The three nuggets would be worth couple hundred dollars at least.

"I took the biggest nugget from the guy who did the talking, well, signing, and gave him the belt. He took the belt and laid it on a stump. Then he made signs that he wanted something else. We didn't understand, but he kept on signing, and I finally took it to mean he wanted a coin. I went back to the tent and brought out my coin bag. I pulled out an eagle and offered it to him. He shook his head, signed that he wanted something smaller. I dug out a half dollar and offered it. He smiled, took it, gave me another nugget that would fetch fifty dollars. Yeah. I hadn't any idea what was going on."

"He fixed the coin in a slit in the end of a stick, walked down the bank about thirty yards or more and poked the stick in the ground. Then he came back, took a bone from his bag, tossed it in the air twice, pointed to each of the other fellas in turn. I'm still wondering what th' hell's going on?

"Well, seems the bone toss decided who got to shoot first. So each shot an arrow at the coin. All of 'em missed, but by a few inches only. We was really impressed. Now the second Indian shot again and actually grazed the coin. The third shot again and missed, but real close. The first Indian, the one that had bargained with me, shot again and, by god, hit the coin square on and sent it flying. They all laughed, real happy.

"The one who hit the coin took the belt from the stump and tied it around his head, grinning ear to ear. They waved to us and waded the stream and walked into the forest, chattering and happy. We had to shake our heads at all this nonsense.

"But we got to thinking. Wouldn't it be something to be that carefree and not be so carried away with owning stuff? I went down the bank and found the coin. Still have it."

"That was the only time we really had any contact with Indians," said Howie. "I wish we could have talked with those fellas. Couldn't they tell us some stories?"

The five fell silent, staring at the dying fire, the glowing embers. Jason looked at the forest canopy across the stream, leaf colors darkening against the evening sky. He looked at Gus.

"What did you tell the miner," said Jason, "about joining the expedition against the mountain Indians?"

"Indians ain't been bothering me," Gus said. "Only Indians I've seen since coming to California last year was in Stockton and those three I told you about. And the woman at the camp up there." He motioned upstream.

Everyone instinctively looked upstream at Gus's gesture. And saw the woman. She waded in the shallows at the willow thicket, looking behind her. She looked around in quick jerks, as if searching for an escape. She left the water and ran toward the five men.

"Help me!" Her thin cotton dress was torn, her hair matted and disheveled, ugly new bruises on her face and an arm. She dropped to her knees at their feet. "Help me," she said softly.

At that moment, the miner who abused her burst through the path in the thicket and strode toward the five.

"Don't touch her!" he shouted.

He staggered and stumbled, found his footing, and came on. She jumped up, cowered, put her hands to her face, backed up and almost fell on Jason.

"Goddam you, don't touch her!" He grabbed her by an arm and pulled her roughly toward him. She stumbled, almost falling.

Jason stood. "By god, that'll do it. Let her go, you son of a bitch." The other four stood.

The man flung her to the ground behind him and advanced on Jason. "You sniveling pup, I'll—"

All Jason's pent-up anger exploded. He destroyed the drunken bully with blows to the head and stomach. The man collapsed to the ground and lay still.

"Oh, my," said Howie, grinning.

Jason helped the woman stand. She looked down at her tormentor, hands on cheeks.

"Now he kill me," she said softly.

Jason looked down at the prostrate man. After a long moment: "No, he won't." He took her hand and led her into the tent. The other four looked at each other, frowning. Paul pursed his lips, raised an eyebrow. Andy shook his head.

A few minutes elapsed, and Jason came through the tent opening, followed by the woman. He wore his coat and pistol belt, and his full pack was on his back. His rifle was slung on a shoulder, and he carried a small bag.

He stopped at the fire circle. "I'm sorry. I've been nothing but trouble. I couldn't stand by any longer. I'll send word somehow, sometime. Sorry to leave you with that," nodding at the man on the ground, still unconscious. He shook hands all around, wished everyone well and received their good wishes.

As he turned to leave, Andy clapped him on the back. "*Vaya con Dios, amigo.* Take care of yourself."

Jason tried without success to smile, turned and walked on the bank, downstream, the woman following.

# Chapter 7

Jason and the woman stood in a thicket at the edge of a clearing. They looked toward what Gus had described as the beginning of a town. A large tent, a corral and small barn of sawn green boards, two frame buildings under construction. Three smaller tents that might have been occupied or used for storage.

"Stay here," Jason said. He shrugged the pack from his shoulders and lowered it to the ground. Adjusting the rifle strap on his shoulder, he walked through the dry grass toward the new settlement. She pulled the pack behind a dense manzanita and sat there, watching him through the branches.

An hour passed, and she decided she had been abandoned. She looked around, desperately. No, he would not leave his pack. Then she saw him striding across the meadow toward her hiding place.

He set a sack on the ground, reached in and pulled out some clothes: a shirt, denim work trousers with large patches at the knees, "blue jeans," the merchant called them, belt and boots, a wool jacket. He handed the clothes to her. She took them, puzzled.

"I got the smallest they had. They probably don't fit, but it's going to get cold soon, and you need something warmer than that dress you're wearing. Do you understand?"

"I understand." She held the clothes, looking back and forth, from the clothes to Jason, confused.

"Well, put them on, and we'll be on our way." *Wherever that is.*

She backed up behind the manzanita as he fumbled with the sack, tying it to his pack with leather straps. He straightened and peered at the settlement, glanced her way to see her tucking shirttails into the pants. She looked up, made eye contact, and he turned away.

She stepped from behind the bush, holding the boots. "I try boots later." He looked down at her moccasins. He took the boots, pushed them into the top of his pack, pulled the drawstring.

"Okay. Ready?" He turned to leave.

She caught his arm. "Thank you." He nodded, shouldered his pack and set out. She fell in behind him.

Jason and the woman sat on each side of a small fire, staring at a plump rabbit carcass skewered on a thin, stripped bough over a low fire. Dripping fat caused a hissing and the brief eruption of tiny tongues of yellow flames. She turned the rod slowly, exposing all sides to the heat from the embers.

He looked up into the treetops, the scant light from the fire illuminating the lower branches of the darkened canopy, creating the illusion of a leafy room. He glanced back at her as she lifted the stick and laid the rabbit on a flat rock beside the fire she had cleaned for the purpose. She pulled the stick from the brown carcass, steam rising as it cooled.

"Careful. Hot," she said.

They pulled bits of meat from the carcass, eating silently, watching each other.

"Okay?" she said.

"Good. Very good." They continued eating, tearing strips of flesh from the carcass until it was clean.

He pulled a bandanna from a pocket and wiped his hands. She picked up a handful of loose soil and dry leaves and rubbed her hands with the grit, then poured water from a canteen over her hands.

He leaned back against a down log, looked long at her as she watched him. She turned and peered into the darkness.

"Tell me," he said.

She looked back at him, straightened. "Friend and I, we happy, not afraid anything. We tell parents we go get acorns, but we want see white people we hear about. We never see before. Before see them, they see us. Two hunters with guns. They say 'stop.' I stop, my friend, she run. They shoot her, kill her. I scare. They take me their camp, then to town call Sacramento. They sell me to man name Hundly. He have store, sell thing for miners."

"What did you do?"

"I clean store, clean house."

"Was he . . . did he—"

"He old man. He not hurt me. His son . . . he . . . bother me. I never know his name."

Jason leaned back, studied her as she stared into the dying fire. She had a pretty face, brown chiseled features, soft in spite of the hardships she had endured. The work shirt and trousers she wore concealed the trim body and small, firm breasts he saw that day in the shallows.

"You speak good English," he said.

She spoke without looking up, still searching the embers. "I have one friend, Sacramento. White lady name Linda, she work for man name Sutter. Something 'bout books, papers. She nice lady, say she teach me English. She from town name Boston. She come in wagon with husband. He die. Linda always sad, say she only happy when she teach me." He saw her tears before she looked aside.

"Why didn't you run away?"

"I try. Two time. They catch me. Hundly son beat me."

"Did you know any other Indians in Sacramento?"

"Yes. They have owners too." She became agitated, leaned forward, stuttered, finding her words. "But Linda say many white people Sacramento say slavery bad, say all Indian slaves must be free! I so happy!

"Some Indian slaves go free. Not me. Hundly tell me he want free me, but son sell me to miner who take me to mountains."

"This is where we saw you?"

"Yes. He bad, bad man. He hurt me." She wiped the tears from a cheek with a hand. "I think I have baby one time. I lose. I want lose. I glad."

Jason touched her hand. "He won't hurt you again. I promise."

Taking his hand in both of hers, she pulled his hand to her chest, held the hand tightly. "Thank you . . . thank you. You good white man. You good man."

She released his hand, and he leaned back against the log.

"What is your name?"

"Tah-nee-hay."

"Tah . . . nee . . . hay."

"Yes. . . . What your name?"

"Jason."

"Jay-son"

They lapsed into silence, watched the dying fire, now glowing embers, searched the darkening canopy. He looked back to her.

"What are we going to do about you?"

She looked into his eyes. "I want go my home."

"And where is that?"

"My home in big valley in high mountains. My valley beautiful. I miss my home so much, I dream my home." She burst into tears, sobbed. "If I don't go my home, I die." She rubbed her face with both hands, dropped her hands into her lap, looked up at the dark canopy, back into his eyes.

"Jay-son. You help me?"

Dusk. Scattered, soft snowflakes swirled overhead. The woman walked about the campground, collecting short dry boughs and sticks. Some she added to the fire, others she piled near the fire circle.

Jayson stood near the fire. He looked up at the ranks of dark gray clouds in the northwest, felt the cold wind that whistled through tall trees, leaves fluttering on branches, separating, flying away. He shivered, pulled up the collar of his coat.

Taking a folded canvas sheet from the bag, he spread it, tied and braced it so that it stretched from the ground at an upward angle, facing the fire. The woman gathered pine needles and dry leaves and laid them for a cushion under the canvas. He watched her pile leaves and needles and other forest detritus on a side of the lean-to to make it as snug as possible. He imitated her on the other side of the enclosure.

Pulling a blanket from the pack, he doubled it and spread it on the needles inside the lean-to. He looked up. The snowflakes had disappeared, but the temperature was still dropping. He shivered.

"It's going to be cold tonight," he said. "I'll keep the fire going." He looked at the lean-to, then at the woman. "You okay?"

"Okay. First time I happy in long, long, long time. I help with fire."

"You climb in first, next to the blanket fold so I can get up to feed the fire."

Kneeling, she raised the blanket, scooted down and pushed her back against the fold. She looked up at him, still standing beside the fire. He picked up a few boughs from the stack and placed them carefully on the fire. She watched him, motionless, waiting.

He knelt and crawled under the awning, sat on the ground and removed his boots. Lifting the top fold of the blanket, he moved over until he lay on the bottom fold. He pushed and pulled the blanket until it covered him. He lay on his back, closed his eyes, exhaled deeply.

She had watched his every move, tense, apprehensive. Now she turned on her side, facing him, pulled the blanket to her chin and closed her eyes.

Jason opened his eyes, blinked, pulled the blanket from his face. The sun had not yet appeared, and the camp was still grey at first light.

He saw the woman stirring the ashes and embers in the fire pit with a stick. Pushing the blanket aside, he sat up, pulled his boots on. He crawled from the lean-to, stood and stretched, grunting.

A fresh dusting of snow had turned the brown land to white, making silvery clumps of bushes. He looked up at snowflakes swirling overhead. He inhaled deeply, at peace.

She turned from the fire, saw him, then returned to raking the ashes. She pushed a brown object the size of a fist from the fire, then another. As he watched, she brushed the objects with a handful of pine needles, then gingerly picked them up and dropped them on the flat rock she had used with the rabbit the day before. She sat down before the fire.

"What's this?" he said.

"White man say 'Indian potato.' It come from root. Good to eat. Come eat now."

Frowning, he sat down beside her. He touched the tuber, jerked his hand back and sucked on the fingers.

"Hot. Be careful," she said.

"Yeah. Ouch." He shook the hand that had touched the root. She smiled.

"This too." She set a handful of small mushrooms on the rock. "This name puffball. We usually cook and make soup, but can eat dry like this."

Pulling a small knife from a boot scabbard, he cut the tuber, releasing a tongue of steam. He speared a piece with the knife and tasted.

"Hmm. I could get used to this. Not bad."

He noticed a small pile of acorns on the ground beside her. "Are we going to eat those? I've never eaten an acorn."

"We no eat unless I find way do them. We make soup and bread, but I cannot do without cooking things."

He ate the last piece of tuber. Picking up a puffball, he examined it, frowning, put it into his mouth and chewed. He swallowed, winced.

"Not so good this way, but we need something eat," she said.

"Yes. And that raises questions. Tahnee, uh, Tah-nee-hay—"

"'Tahnee' okay, you like."

"The weather is turning colder, and now this snow."

"This early snow, but I think more snow come quick."

"The point is, we're not prepared for cold and snow. How far to your home?"

"I not know. I need find Indian people tell us. It many days away, but snow make it hard. And . . . and . . ."

"What?"

"Valley where we live in high mountains, most winter very cold, much snow. Sometime my people, we go down to lower place, you say 'foothills,' where not so cold, not so much snow. But if winter not so bad, not so cold, not so much snow, we stay in our valley during winter. You understand?"

"Yes."

"I don't know if my people stay in my valley this winter, or if they in foothills now."

"Hmm. That's a problem. Well, we'll have to think about that. But whatever we do, we're going to have to find someplace soon to get supplies, some blankets, maybe horses."

"Where we go?"

"We could go to Stockton, but that's a long way." He pondered. "One of the miners at my camp talked about a town south of here named Mariposa. Ever hear of it?"

"No."

He searched the canopy. "We have no choice. Tomorrow we'll head south. We should meet people on the trail who can tell us about this town."

The snowfall increased during the night, and the temperature dropped as a brisk north wind threatened to demolish the canvas lean-to.

They broke camp at first light. Though Jason set a course that would take them lower in the foothills, they could not escape the heavy blowing snow and deep drifts. The trail was no longer visible.

They walked silently for hours. As the light began to fail, Jason led Tahnee into a thick cluster of pines where there was a space mostly free of snow and sheltered from the wind. Dropping his pack, he collected stones for a fire circle while Tahnee gathered sticks and short boughs for the fire. He pulled the fat squirrel he had shot earlier from his pack and gave it to her.

While she worked at the fire pit, Jason set up the canvas lean-to, collected needles and dry leaves for a mattress, then pushed needles and detritus into the sides of the lean-to. He pulled the blanket from the pack and spread it on the needles.

Tahnee built the fire of twigs and pine needles, then carefully placed sticks and short boughs on the flames. He knelt beside her, shivering. She looked over at him. "Almost done," she said. "You cold." He nodded.

She had placed half a dozen stones in the center of the fire. Now she raked the fire from the stones and placed the skinned squirrel on them. She added small sticks around the stones that caught fire quickly.

"I not find good stick to cook, so use rocks. Okay, I think."

He nodded, still shivering. They sat in silence. Tahnee moved the squirrel around on the stones to cook it evenly. Jason watched, alternately warming his hands over the fire and hugging them under his armpits.

She prodded the squirrel flesh with a sharp stick and twisted. The flesh pulled away. "Okay," she said. She skewered the carcass with the stick and placed it on a flat rock outside the fire circle. She jabbed the flesh with the stick and pulled away a slice, offered it to him.

He took the meat with unsteady hands, ate it slowly. "Yes, good." His teeth chattered.

They ate quickly, tearing pieces from the carcass until it was stripped clean.

"Now, you go bed," she said. "I put wood on fire and get more sticks." He started to protest, but she pushed him toward the lean-to.

She went outside the circle of firelight to relieve herself, then gathered sticks from the clear space under the pines. She built up the fire and added to the pile near the fire pit. The light snowfall during their meal now increased, and the icy north wind blew harder, flapping the top canvas of the lean-to.

Tahnee knelt and crawled inside the shelter. She raised the blanket, slid in beside Jason. He lay on his side, facing her.

"Never felt this cold," he said, teeth chattering.

She slid over, pressed against him. "I warm," she said. Her head lay against his chest, under his chin, and his face was in her hair. She raised her chin, and he felt her warm breath on his neck.

He stopped shivering. Putting his arm around her back, he pulled her against his body. She raised her chin, whispered in his ear. “You warm now?”

He raised her chin, looked into her eyes, kissed her. “I warm now.”

# Chapter 8

Tahnee stood with arms extended, turning round and round, smiling and giggling. A swarm of orange butterflies flew about her head and covered her arms and swirled about her face. She laughed out loud.

"I never see before!"

Jason extended his hands as the Monarchs settled on his arms and shoulders.

They stood on a low rising in rugged foothills looking down on the collection of tents and new frame buildings that comprised the town of Mariposa. A small creek snaked through the town, the thin flow bordered with spikey ice. A scattering of ponderosa pines and gray pines on the slopes gave way to blue oaks and gray oaks in and about the town.

"Let's have a look." Jason headed down the hill, Tahnee following.

As they walked in the only street, passersby turned and watched the two, this miner and his Indian woman. *His* Indian woman? Jason could almost feel their minds churning and smiled to himself.

He stopped in front of a frame house identified by the sign as "Teddy's Room and Board." He knocked.

The door opened. "Yep?" said a grizzled, frowning face.

"Do you have a room for a few days?"

The man looked over his shoulder at Tahnee who stood in the street, watching the exchange.

"She with you?"

"She is."

"We don't take no Indians."

Jason frowned. "You don't take no Indians," he said softly. "Why is it you 'don't take no Indians'?"

"We just don't take no Indians."

Jason paused, glared. "She's housebroke and knows how to use a knife and fork."

"Don't matter." He pointed down the street. "Go down there to Billy's place. He'll take you. He's got a Indian wife." The scowl made it clear that he did not approve of the union.

Jason straightened, inhaled deeply, exhaled, staring at the man, pondering, trying to decide whether to pity him or flatten him. He turned, took Tahnee by the arm, and they walked away. She looked back at the man who still leaned out from his doorway, watching them.

They passed the general store and a feed store, stopped at a small building with a hand-printed sign on the wall beside the door: "Billy's Rooms." Jason knocked.

The door opened, and there stood an Indian woman. She was short and stout, with a round, pleasant face, probably in her mid-twenties. She wore a simple, cotton dress. Her hair was tied up in a bun, loose strands in every direction. She wiped her hands on a towel.

Jason smiled. "Can we get a room for a few days?"

"Sure can." She moved aside, and Jason stepped in. She held out an arm, motioning to Tahnee. "Come in, missy." Tahnee smiled and walked through the door. The woman closed it.

"Now, will you be wanting just the room, or will you be wanting meals?"

"Meals with the room for now," said Jason, "as long as we're strangers here. We'll see how it goes."

"Okay, let me know if you want to go off meals," she said. "I'm Bess, and I'll be taking care of you. Billy's my husband. You won't see a lot of him. He works at the livery and keeps all sorts of hours."

"Nice to meet you, Bess. I'm Jason."

She turned to Tahnee. "And you, Missy?"

"Tah-nee-hay. Jason call me 'Tahnee.'"

"Tah . . . nee . . . hay." She pursed her lips, pondering. "You are Miwok, I think."

Tahnee beamed. "Yes! You know my people?"

"Not really. We get all sorts here, miners and traders and cowboys and farmers. And local people." She smiled at Jason. "Local people, that's people like Tah-nee-hay and me."

"Where your home," said Tahnee.

"Right here in Mariposa."

"I mean—"

"I know what you mean, honey. But I never knew any other home. I was took when I was too little to remember. My husband got me from a trader who wouldn't say where he got me. My husband's always been good to me, so I'm happy. He's old enough to be my daddy, and that's okay. As for where I come from, two Indian men at different times said I looked Paiute. I guess that's possible. They said the Paiute live mostly on the other side of the mountains. I don't think about it. Too late. I'm not unhappy. This is the only life and the only place I know.

"Anyway." She hefted Jason's pack. "Let's get you to your room. C'mon." She led the way down a hall, opened a door and deposited the pack inside. "This is your room. Okay?"

"This will be fine," said Jason. Tahnee walked in, sat on the bed.

"Supper in about an hour. That okay?"

"That's fine," said Jason, "I could eat that old horse tied out front." Bess smiled, backed out, and closed the door.

On their journey from the placer to Mariposa, Jason and Tahnee had subsisted for days on the occasional rabbit and squirrel and whatever natural foods Tahnee could find. They agreed that Bess's supper of roast beef, boiled potatoes, beans and cornbread, apple cobbler and strong hot black coffee was a feast and a forecast of meals to come.

The dining room contained but four tables, two at the windows and two against the wall opposite the kitchen door. Dishes and linens were stacked on a long service table. The space was warmed by a wood-burning potbellied stove in the center of the room that radiated heat. A rustic couch in the corner opposite the windows was the only reminder that this was once a sitting room.

When they converted their home to a guesthouse, Billy cut the door in the wall between the sitting-dining room and the kitchen. They also built an extension at the back, which added two bedrooms, the larger for Billy and Bess and a small guest room, bringing the number of guest rooms to four.

Only one of the other tables was occupied this evening by a bewhiskered oldster who kept his own counsel and said nothing during the entire meal but an occasional grunt to Bess that served as an acknowledgement of her attentions. She seemed not be bothered.

*****

A cold north wind blew every day for the next week. Temperatures dropped well below freezing every night and hovered around freezing during the day. Snow alternated with sleet, and the snowpack increased daily.

What to do? They found Billy and Bess congenial and helpful and Bess's meals tasty and ample. Billy introduced Jason to an honest merchant who Billy said would give him the best price for his gold dust. Soon Jason was asking Billy to handle the transaction when he needed cash.

Jason and Tahnee sat often at their table by the window in the dining room, warmed by the potbellied wood stove, drinking coffee and watching the storm outside. This morning they were alone in the room.

They talked about their options. They could do what they had intended: buy the outfit they needed and strike out for Tahnee's home now. Or they could stay at Billy's until winter broke and set out for Tahnee's home at the first hint of spring. As they lingered at their window, watching the snowfall, the latter appeared the only viable choice.

Jason sipped his coffee, set the cup on the table. He studied Tahnee's face as she stared through the window at the storm depositing a fresh dusting to the frozen yard, shrubs appearing as short domes. Her chin rested in a hand, and she leaned toward the frosted window glass. She had washed her black hair that morning, and it shone in the weak light from the window.

She glanced at him, noticed his stare. She frowned. "What?"

He simply stared. After a moment: "Bess called you a Miwok."

"Yes, Miwok people live all over country in mountains around my home. Not all Miwok are same. We call ourselves, people who live my home, we call ourselves Ahwahneechee. We call our home, our valley, Ah-wah-nee. "

"What do white men call your valley?"

"They never see! No white man know our valley. Maybe you be first white man see our valley."

He looked through the window. Snow blew almost horizontally, obscuring the view beyond the garden.

"We'll see." He stood. "I need to find out whether this expedition we heard about is still in the works." He took the coat from the back of his chair and put it on. Leaning over, he kissed her lightly. She ducked her head, glanced around furtively, looked up at him and smiled.

She turned in her chair and watched him walk into the hall, then heard the front door close.

Outside, Jason raised the collar of his coat and pulled the hat lower. He walked down the street, leaning into the blowing snow, wondering where he would likely find information about the prospect of a military force gathering. Since the affair seemed to him a lunatic undertaking, he decided that he should listen to conversation at the saloon they passed after the encounter at Teddy's Room and Board.

He pushed the door of the Hideout open and stepped inside. The stale odor of tobacco smoke, alcohol and unwashed bodies assaulted him. The place was crowded at late morning. All of the chairs around the half dozen tables were filled, and a dozen men stood at the bar. Strange, thought Jason, saloons weren't usually busy till late afternoon or later.

Shaking the snow off his coat, he walked to the bar. A couple of men with boots hooked on the foot rail nodded to him and made room.

The smiling barkeep stepped over. "What can I do ya for, friend?"

"Whisky and conversation, if you're willing."

"I can do that, on both counts." He picked up a glass from the cabinet behind him, deposited it on the counter before Jason and poured. "What would you like to converse about?"

Jason picked up the glass, raised it in salute to the bartender, and sipped. "I've heard something about somebody in Mariposa getting a force up to go against some troublesome Indians. Any truth in that?"

Rough-dressed men on each side of Jason glanced at him. The bartender smiled broadly. "There is indeed some truth in that. You're at the right place at the right time. Most of the men in the room are not here to drink my fine whiskey; they're here to listen to James Savage talk about that very subject. He'll be here shortly."

"Savage. What's he got against the Indians?"

The man standing next to Jason at the bar raised his glass and emptied it, turned to Jason. "I can tell you that. I know Mr. Savage real well. Things been heating up some time. Mr. Savage has always been a friend to the Indians. He's been trading with them for years. He learned their languages. Hell, they like him so much he's been made a chief of some tribes. He's even got Indians wives, five of 'em!

"It was all peaceful, but some Indians, mostly the Miwok and Chinchillas, got all upset with whites moving into their country, you know, working the streams, cutting down the acorn oaks, hunting and scaring off the game and the like. The Indians complained to Savage, but he couldn't do nothing about that. So the Indians began raiding the placers and trading posts, even Savage's own posts, killing people and stealing stuff."

"Savage don't really want a war. " It was the man on Jason's other side who had listened to the exchange. "He just wants the Indians to understand that things have changed, and they have to accept that. He, and a lot of other people, want to convince the Indians that they have to move out of the mountains and down to a reservation in the valley that's been set aside for them."

A man who had been sitting at a table near the bar, listening to the conversation, could restrain himself no longer. He stood and pushed into the group. "Lemme tell you something to show you how smart Mr. Savage is. I work for him. He decided that he would show the Indians how strong the Americans are. He's had Indians working for him in the placers a long time. They pan for gold, he gives them a trinket or piece of cloth for their dust. Everybody's happy.

"Now he has to go to San Francisco from time to time to put his gold in safekeeping. Here's the good part. He decides to take some Indian leaders with him to show them how powerful the whites are, and that there are a hell of a lot of whites! The chiefs were impressed, especially with the whites' whiskey, and they were drunk most of the time.

"One chief named José became so drunk that he lost it. He told Mr. Savage that the Indians could beat the whites any time they wanted to. He said the whites in San Francisco would never come to the mountains to help fight them. Mr. Savage was so angry he knocked him down." He snorted.

The speaker, wide-eyed at his own story, continued. "Okay, listen, I'm almost through. When they got back to Mariposa, Mr. Savage called a meeting of all the chiefs around. He said he had just been to San Francisco where the whites were more numerous than the wasps and the ants. If there ever was to be war between the Americans and the tribes, every Indian in the war would be killed, and that would not be good, he said.

"Mr. Savage thought José had learned his lesson, so he called on him to confirm what he had said. José was sober now, and he surprised Mr. Savage. José said that he had sure enough seen many Americans, but those people were so caught up in making money and drinking whiskey that they would not come help the Mariposa whites fight the Indians. All the Indians cheered. Another chief, José Rey of the Chowchillas, said the Indians should make war on the whites. Right now. Mr. Savage was surprised at all this and walked out. That's pretty much where we stand now. The damn Indians want to make war on us."

Jason frowned. "But if the whites are moving into the Indians' country, then—"

"Here he is!" someone near the door shouted. Applause and cheering erupted as Major James Savage and another man walked into the saloon. The noise diminished gradually as Savage waited.

"Here's where we stand," said Savage. "Most of you will know our Sheriff, Joe Burney here. We've been working together on this. We appealed to Governor McDougal for his support, and the state of California has authorized the formation of a force of 204 volunteers to guarantee the safety of the southern mines." Cheers and fist pumping from the crowd.

"You've probably heard about the federal commissioners that are negotiating treaties with the local and mountain tribes. They have outlined plans for a reservation on the Fresno River near the foothills." More cheers and shouts.

"The commissioners have secured the assistance of Mission Indians to persuade the mountain tribes to move to the reservation. Any who refuse to move will be considered hostiles, and the battalion will conduct operations against them. We expect that most of the tribes will see the futility of resistance, but there will be some who likely may not, particularly the Chowchillas and the Miwoks in the high mountains.

"Beginning tomorrow morning, we're signing on volunteers for the Mariposa Battalion in the sheriff's office. If you are determined to protect your families from the hostiles, I expect to see you there." Savage and the sheriff went out amidst cheers and raucous yells.

The men leaning on the bar turned around, picked up their glasses. One of the men raised his glass, emptied it, set it gently on the counter top. "He's the man." He turned to the others. "Did you know that Jim Savage was with the Fremont battalion in the Bear Flag? Yep. He fought the Mexicans and helped set up the California Republic. He's the man to keep all this going. First, the Mexicans, now the Indians. Yep."

Jason sipped his whiskey. He listened to the conversation of a trio nearby that leaned against the bar. It seems that one of the men had come from San Francisco with the federal commissioners. He said that the commissioners actually were sympathetic with the mountain Indians. The commissioners, he said, think that the Indians might be justified in wishing to remain on their ancestral lands. At the commissioners' insistence, the Governor had instructed Major Savage to hold off any action against all tribes until the commissioners had studied the situation. Savage had not mentioned this restraint to the mob in the Hideout.

One of the men at the bar who had listened without comment countered that these eastern government fellas had not lost family members and property to the hostilities of the mountain Indians. All murmured their agreement.

The barkeep finished serving a customer, walked over to Jason, leaned over the bar, grinning. "Now, you were saying?"

Jason raised his glass, emptied it, turned and followed the exodus still pouring through the front door.

Jason and Tahnee sat at their usual table by the window. The snowfall had ended, but for a few lacy flakes swirling above the yard. Empty lunch dishes were stacked in the middle of the table. Jason told her about the gathering at the Hideout, about Major Savage and the fledgling Mariposa Battalion.

Then they sipped their coffee in silence, occasionally glancing at the two men sitting at a table near the door.

"Who are Mission Indians?" Tahnee said.

"I asked the same question at the Hideout. Seems they are members of tribes that were forced by the Spanish and Mexicans to become Christians and live around Missions. They gave up all the old ways and became more white than Indian. Now some of them work for the commissioners, talking with the mountain tribes, trying to persuade them to move to the reservation. They are supposed to tell the tribes that they will have all on the reservation they need. Food, clothing, a place to live, everything."

"Hmm. I never heard of Mission Indians."

The two men at the nearby table had eaten their lunch in silence, occasionally glancing at Jason and Tahnee, obviously eavesdropping. Now the two stood. As they struggled into coats, they looked over at Jason and Tahnee. "Saw you at the Hideout," one said to Jason. He looked pointedly at Tahnee. "You joining the battalion?" He grinned.

Jason pondered a moment. "Just passing through." The speaker smirked, followed his companion into the hall.

Jason stared at the doorway, wondering whether he should have responded, whether he should even now go outside and knock him senseless. He decided that he would let it go. He turned back to Tahnee.

"Savage talked about hostiles and peaceful tribes, but mentioned the names of only two, the Chowchillas and the Yosemites. Do you know anything about them?"

"The Yosemites are my people. That is what some of the tribes around my valley call us. And that is what whites call us."

"He said these two tribes were most likely to resist the battalion. I think I will like the Chowchillas and Yosemites. But I will fear for them. This force that Savage is putting together will include a lot of Indian-haters. They will have better weapons than your people."

"We must warn them, Jay-son. Can we go soon?"

He looked out the window. The swirling flakes had turned to a steady snowfall, adding a new dusting to the pack.

"The battalion surely won't set out in this. There'll be plenty of activity in Mariposa when Savage decides to make his move. We'll try to get the jump on them and stay ahead. I've bought all the gear we need and told Billy at the livery that I'll give him a one-day notice before picking up the horses and pack mule. Everything's ready, but it would be foolish to travel in the dead of winter. I hope Savage is of the same opinion.

"Do you know the way to your home from here?"

"I never go home from here, but we will see other Indian in mountain, and they can help us. Jay-son, maybe my people not in my valley. I told you that sometime when winter very cold and much snow, my people move lower in what you call foothills."

"Hmm." He pondered. "Savage said they were having some problems with Chinchillas and Yosemites. If he's right, your people, at least some of them, may not be far away."

He stood. "Now, let's bundle up and get some air and exercise. I'm getting too used to warm houses and sitting."

They returned to their room and collected coats, scarves, gloves and hats. Pulling them on as they walked in the hall toward the front door, they saw Bess coming from the dining room with her hands full of dishes.

"Your cooking too good," said Tahnee. "I never want leave dining room."

"Glad you like it. Going out, are you?"

They stopped in the hall. "Out for a walk and conversation. I don't suppose you've heard anything about the battalion lately, have you?" Jason said.

"Nope, but I've seen a bunch of fellas that looks like they're fixing on being part of it. Some look okay, but some look like drifters who want something to do, and they're happy to do it against Indians."

"I'm afraid you're probably right." He put his hat on and walked toward the front door, Tahnee following.

Outside, they buttoned coats and raised collars. They set out toward the town center. It would take all of two minutes to reach the other end of the main street, if they should chose to do so. The town had grown with the opening of the southern mines, but it was still small and exhibiting birth pangs, tents only gradually being replaced with frame structures.

They strolled. Jason looked down, as if studying the sidewalk. He frowned. It all seemed so unreal. After leaving Independence, he was adrift, with no direction, without purpose, unconcerned about the moment or the morrow. Now everything had changed, and Tahnee was the reason. He had been reluctant to believe so at first. Every time he thought of Tahnee, images of Jessica, and Christian and Nicole obscured her face, shame and guilt flooded over him, and he had to struggle to hold back the tears. Then Tahnee would speak or smile or touch him, and he was alone with her.

Most days, with no obligation but to wait and watch, they retired early and rose late. Closing the door on the unheated bedroom, they shed their clothes quickly, threw them on chairs, fell into bed and pulled up covers, shivering. Since being shocked by his cold hands on her naked body the first night here, she thereafter rubbed his hands in hers until his were warm. Then they explored each other's body and made love and lay close, arms and legs intertwined, and slept as if they were alone in the universe.

"Jay-son?"

He looked up from the sidewalk at her, smiled. Taking her arm, he pulled her to him. Passersby stared. A couple, an older man and woman, stopped when they had passed and watched. The man leaned over and spoke softly to the woman. She nodded, and they resumed walking.

At town center, in front of the Hideout, Jason stopped. "Do you want to come in?" She shook her head. "Don't go far. I won't be long." He walked inside behind a scruffy character that might have satisfied Bess's comment about drifters.

Tahnee leaned against the Hideout wall, her eyes closed and face up, enjoying the weak sun that had appeared the moment they left the boarding house.

"Well, would you look at this, Bonney?" Her eyes popped open to see the two men standing in front of her.

"Um, *um,*" said the other. "Looks tasty to me, Bart." Both smiled.

"Yeah, tasty is right. Ya think we outta get us a piece of this little purty?"

"Now that sounds like—"

Bonney stopped short when he realized that a scowling man had stepped up slowly behind Bart. Bart noticed Bonney looking behind him. He whirled around and was nose to nose with Jason.

"Git outta my face!" said Bart.

"Be on your way, arsehole," Jason said softly, "and all is well."

"What's this? You interested in this woman? You're too late, she's ours and we—"

Jason grabbed Bart by the coat collar at his neck and almost lifted him off the ground. Bart wrenched Jason's hand from his coat and swung wildly at him. Jason ducked and punched him hard in the stomach. When Bart folded forward, gasping, Jason landed a hard right to the head, propelling him off the plank sidewalk. He crumpled in the soft slush of the road.

Jason turned to Bonney, who appeared poised to come at him, and raised a warning finger in his face. Bonney backed off, walked cautiously around Jason and knelt beside Bart.

Bonney looked up at Jason. "This ain't finished, mister."

"Up to you." He took Tahnee's arm, and they walked in the direction of Bess's place.

They strolled in silence. She looked up at him, expecting, but when he said nothing, she asked what he learned at the Outpost.

"Seems they have about half the number of volunteers they want and expect to have no trouble getting the rest. Some hot-bloods are eager to set out, but Savage and the other leaders know they can't leave until a break in the weather. They're pretty upset that the cold and snow don't seem to have prevented the hostiles, as they call them, from raiding placers and trading posts. Some of Savage's own posts have been hit again. He's hopping mad since he thought he had the Indians under his thumb.

"The mountain Indians have been so successful with their raiding that some bands that had given up and were living on the Fresno River reservation have returned to the mountains. That makes them hostiles.

Savage is furious and anxious to get the battalion moving.

"The volunteers are likely just as anxious. There's probably some hell raisers and drifters among them, but the word is that most of them are men who are taking time off from their usual labors, miners, cowboys, shopkeepers, and will need to get back to working for a living as soon as possible. Seems that some have personally suffered from Indian attacks. These especially will have no love for Indians."

# Chapter 9

For weeks, light snow fell intermittently, and travel outside Mariposa was a risk. Jason rode into the foothills occasionally, looking for evidence of a break in the weather, but snowfall was heavier at the higher elevations, and he had to report to Tahnee that they could not yet leave.

The weather did not prevent Savage and a volunteer force from conducting operations against tribes in the foothills. He promised the Indians that they would be provided with food and shelter and everything they needed on the reservation. Some bands agreed to move, but others resisted. Savage's force attacked the hostiles, for so they were considered when they resisted, burning villages and destroying food supplies, leaving the Indians with no option but to withdraw deeper and higher in the mountains or move to the reservation. Most, with their goods and homes destroyed, chose the reservation.

Jason heard all the talk about the campaign against the hostiles at the Outpost. Volunteers were heady at their success and looked forward to the completion of the battalion's organization so they could embark on the final removal, or annihilation, of the Yosemites and other holdouts in the high mountains.

When the weather permitted, Jason and Tahnee walked in the snowy meadows and trails around Mariposa. In town, they stopped occasionally in the café for lunch and visited with Billy at the livery where he tended their two horses and the mule.

On one particular morning, they sat on hay bales in the livery barn, sipping hot coffee, listening to Billy's tales of California before the gold rush in '49. He had washed up on the shore, so he said, in Los Angeles a lifetime ago when he was a young sprout. He drifted northward, worked on ranches, invariably got a wandering itch, and moved on, footloose, with no idea of what he wanted to do or where he wanted to be.

"What brought you to Mariposa?" Jason said.

"Worked on a ranch right here, before there was a Mariposa. Been here fifteen years now."

"You always move. Why you stay here?" said Tahnee.

He smiled. "Bess. I bought her from an old trader who was passing through. He needed cash more than he needed a woman. When I got Bess, my wandering days were over. She's my rock and my anchor."

"I like Bess," said Tahnee. Billy looked up, smiled.

They sat silent, sipping their coffee.

"Heard any talk about the battalion lately?" Jason said.

Billy stood. "Come 'ere." He beckoned toward the door. Jason and Tahnee followed him outside, behind the livery. They walked a few steps into the meadow.

Billy faced south. "Feel that?" They looked south and felt the slightest hint of a breeze on their faces.

"Oh," said Tahnee, "little bit warm."

"Yep. As to your question, nope, I hadn't heard anything about the battalion moving, but we'll soon hear some talk. We got a break in the weather coming soon. It might not be the end of winter, but it's a break. Savage knows the seasons hereabouts. He'll have to decide whether this means the end of the snows or whether it's just a breather."

Tahnee looked at Jason.

He nodded. "Billy, looks like we should be leaving in a day or two. Can you sell the rest of my dust for me?"

"I can do that. Matter of fact, it might be a good time to sell. Some of the volunteers are miners, and they won't be selling any dust as long as the battalion's on campaign. Price might go up.

"Look here. If I was you and didn't want nobody to know where I was going, I would go in the opposite direction from where I was going. Make sense? Look." He pointed eastward. "That's where you want to go, but you don't want nobody to know you're going that way. So if I was you, I would go that way." He pointed westward. "If anybody asks, I'll tell 'em you got tired of California, and you're heading for Stockton and home. How's that?"

"Sounds good to me," said Jason.

"Soon as you're out of sight of town, turn north a few miles, then head east and pass well north of town. Keep headin' toward the morning sun, and you'll soon be in the mountains."

The next two days were still cold, but the soft, southerly breeze persisted, and trickles of melt water ran from snowdrifts.

Early morning of the second day, Jason and Tahnee said goodbye to Bess and Billy on their front porch. They mounted and rode westward on the trail toward Stockton. Jason held the lead of the pack mule. Turning in the saddle, they waved to Bess and Billy who returned the wave.

They rode in silence until Mariposa was indistinguishable from the line of trees that marked the edge of the valley. Leaving the trail and turning north, they rode through a landscape of snow and slush, appearing as a frothy sea. Yet, tiny bright green shoots broke the icy cover in all directions. Jason remembered when he and Andy and Paul had crossed this plain last summer, and the grass was as tall as their horses' bellies.

After a couple of hours, they turned eastward. The sun was directly overhead now in a clear cobalt sky. Ahead, the mountains loomed, high peaks, snow-capped and rugged, and below, a belt of dark blue and purple.

Jason and Tahnee rode side by side. He glanced at her. Her hand was at her mouth, tears marking her cheek.

"What's wrong?" he said.

She looked at him, lowered her hand. "I go home."

"I think we're going to be okay," Jason said. They had camped last night on the edge of the plain, a spot free of snow though a layer of slush still lay on most of the land.

Now they rode in the lower reaches of the foothills on a trail through forests of digger pines and sugar pines. Snow clung to needles on branches and still covered the land, but the snow was icy, indicating that the melt had begun. As they ascended, the snowpack was deeper, and there was less evidence of melting. The temperature dropped with the increase in elevation.

By the time the sun lay on the western horizon, they had ridden higher into a snow-covered land that showed no evidence of melt. The temperature had plummeted.

They found a flat open place in a stand of pine and birch that they agreed silently would do for the night. They set about making camp, having long since adopted a separation of duties. Jason set up the small canvas tent, pushed the packs and bags inside at the back and laid out the blankets. Then he made a fire circle of stones near the tent opening. Meanwhile Tahnee prepared the evening meal from their packs.

Jason led the horses and mule to a site behind the tent he had spotted earlier. He hobbled the animals in a tight grove of young birch trees that was backed by a rock face. The grove and the wall should provide some protection from the wind. He fashioned a pen of poles tied with short lengths of rope and hoped the animals would mistake the rough enclosure for a corral.

He hurried around the tent, hunched over from the cold, and hovered over the fire beside Tahnee. A pot of beef and beans bubbled in the embers.

Tahnee looked up at him. "Not ready."

"Good. I saw some deer in the trees back behind where I put the animals. I'm gonna see if I spooked 'em." He reached into the tent, pulled the rifle from its case and verified that it was loaded. "I'll just be a few minutes."

Ten minutes passed. Tahnee's head came up at a shot. She looked in the direction of the sound. A few minutes later, Jason emerged from the forest, dragging a small deer on the snow.

"Saw two does, a fawn and a yearling. I got the yearling. Should keep us in meat as long as we're in this camp, and I'll pack the rest." He stooped inside the tent, opened a bag and pulled out a short rope. Tying the rope to the hind legs of the deer, he pulled it to a large oak. He threw the rope over an almost horizontal limb and pulled the deer a few feet off the ground.

"Come eat now, finish after," Tahnee said.

He flexed his back, bent over the fire and added some sticks to the flames. Squatting with a grunt, he took the plate Tahnee offered. They ate in silence.

"Weather more cold," she said.

"Yeah, it'll be warmer in the sunshine tomorrow."

When they finished eating, Tahnee took his empty plate and carried all the dishes to a nearby rivulet that flowed in a depression gorged with small ferns and washed them.

Jason walked to the hanging deer, pulled a knife from a belt scabbard and dressed the carcass. That done, he pulled the rope until the carcass was out of any carnivore's reach. Pushing the offal aside, he covered it with leaves.

He walked back to the tent where Tahnee was waiting. He shivered. "If we can't sit by this fire all night, you're going to have to warm me up."

"I can do."

While Jason saddled the horses, Tahnee washed the breakfast dishes. She shook the water from the dishes, walked back to camp.

She stopped beside the fire circle, still holding the dishes that dripped on the embers, causing a hissing and tiny eruptions of steam. She looked up. The deep blue sky at first light had turned a dark gray, almost black in the north. The whisper of a breeze at daybreak had changed to a brisk, cold north wind.

"Jay-son." He turned to her, his hands on his horse's cinch. "I think we stay here. Snow coming. Much snow."

"The weather is fine." He tightened the cinch. "We need to move to stay ahead of the battalion. I'll just get that yearling. I'll need to do some butchering at noon stop. "

"Jay-son! Listen me! I know weather here better than you. Much snow come tonight. We need get ready. You hear me?"

He stopped, pondered, staring at his saddle. "Okay, pretty lady, I suppose you do know more than me about these mountains. What do you suggest?"

"We make u-ma-cha."

"Uma-what?"

"Listen. I tell you. We need hurry, or we freeze tonight. Bring axe."

As they walked into the forest behind camp, Tahnee described the Yosemite dwelling they called u-ma-cha. She showed him a stand of saplings that were straight and tall. While he cut the saplings and stripped them, she found downed incense cedars and pulled long slabs of bark from the trunks.

After some hours had passed, Jason said they should stop to eat something. She replied that they must continue; they could eat later.

"We no can work on u-ma-cha in dark," she said.

By mid-afternoon, they had gathered the materials they needed. They took the tent down and moved packs aside. Raising the poles in a circle around the fire pit, they positioned pole bottoms about five feet from the pit with the tops leaning into each other.

As snowflakes swirled about the treetops, they pushed slabs of cedar bark into the detritus on the ground, leaning them against the poles. She showed him how to wedge the second row of slabs above the first, then the next higher row tightly against the slabs below since they did not find any vines to tighten the bark against the poles, the usual practice when building an u-ma-cha. They continued adding rows of bark until the dwelling sides were covered to the top. A low narrow opening for an entrance was left on the south side of the structure.

By the time they finished, snow flurries had increased to a steady fall pushed by a fierce north wind. The snow quickly covered footprints and supplies and packs near the u-ma-cha.

"I work here," she said. "You take care animals."

"Yes, ma'am." He smiled. She cuffed him on his arm.

She brushed snow from the supplies and cooking gear and moved them inside the u-ma-cha. Then she walked about the site, kicking snow aside, collecting boughs and sticks and stacked them just inside the opening. Walking to where Jason had stripped the poles, she picked up small limbs he had removed and added these to the stack in the u-ma-cha.

Jason fed each of the animals a bit of grain, checked the hobbles. He tested the poles that enclosed the pen and found them secure. When he walked from the protection of the grove and rock face, the full force of the storm hit him, the heavy snow flying almost horizontal in the freezing wind.

At the u-ma-cha, he stooped and stepped inside. He straightened, looked around, wide-eyed. He was suddenly warm. The fire crackled and softly illuminated the interior. He saw the saddles and blankets that Tahnee had placed against the wall. Sitting down beside her, he grunted with the effort, exhaled heavily.

"You okay?" she said.

He leaned over and kissed her cheek. "I'm okay. In fact, I feel pretty good. First time I have been warm since leaving Bess's dining room." He looked up at the peak where the smoke from the fire filtered out through the spaces between poles and bark. "You are a marvel."

He frowned, stirred the embers with a stick. *I started to add, "my little sweetheart," but it caught in my throat. Will I ever get over it? Should I get over it?*

Tahnee had watched him staring silently into the fire. "I don't think you okay."

He reached for her and pulled her to him. He kissed her lips hard, parted and kissed her again, softly. "You are a marvel, my little sweetheart. Do you know 'sweetheart?'"

She frowned. "I think so. It mean someone you love?"

"Yes. That's what it means."

"You . . . love me?"

"You saved my life, and I love you for that."

She frowned, cocked her head. "I no save you life. Why you say that?"

"I'll explain someday. Right now, let's build up the fire and go to bed. Okay?"

She leaned over and kissed him lightly. "Okay . . . sweetheart." She laughed out loud.

First light. Jason rubbed his eyes, gently pushed the blanket down, hoping not to awaken Tahnee. Then he saw her, fully clothed, bending over the fire, sparks rising as she lay sticks around the coffee pot. She removed a bucket from the embers and set it near the u-ma-cha opening.

He rose to his knees, reached and grabbed her at the waist and pulled her sprawling on her back beside him. He caressed her breast, leaned down and kissed her.

She smiled, kissed him lightly. Pushing him away, she sat up. "No time. I busy." She stood, pointed at the bucket. "Water for horse. I melt snow." She picked up the ax from the stack of packs. "We need meat. Deer freeze."

He stood and dressed, mumbling to himself: "Thought I got a woman, but got a supervisor instead."

She frowned. "What you say?"

He smiled, leaned over and kissed her cheek. "Nothing, my little sweetheart boss."

"What mean 'boss?'"

"Never mind." He pulled on his coat. "I busy." He took the ax from her, picked up the bucket of water, stooped and went out.

He stepped into a foot of new snow. There was only a hint of a breeze, and no snowfall, but the cold crept under the scarf wrapped around his ears and burned his cheeks. He felt the deer carcass. Stone hard. He leaned the ax against the tree and walked to the animals.

His horse nickered at his approach. The three animals appeared to have come through the storm all right. He set the bucket on the ground, and the three jockeyed for a drink. He gave grain to each and rubbed each with a piece of sacking. Maybe he would try to walk them in the afternoon.

He filled the bucket with snow, packing it repeatedly, then walked to the hanging deer carcass. He untied the rope holding the deer, lowered it and re-tied it. Picking up the ax, he hacked off a slab of flesh. That done, he untied the rope, pulled the carcass higher on the limb and tied the rope.

Inside the u-ma-cha, Jason set the bucket on the ground adjacent to the fire. Tahnee put the venison on a flat rock beside the fire to thaw. She had already fashioned a three-foot long thin pole atop two forked sticks for roasting the meat.

Jason had hardly settled before the fire when the storm returned with a fury. The wind whistled in the bare branches that whipped and clicked, and the snow beat against the walls of the u-ma-cha. They built up the fire and watched the snow blowing outside the opening.

When they had finished eating and putting dishes aside, Jason pulled Tahnee to the bed and tugged blankets over them. They struggled to remove clothing under the cover, laughing at the effort, then explored each other's body, Tahnee warming Jason's cold hands, the intensity and sounds of their lovemaking an echo of the violence of the storm outside, knowing no one could hear. Afterwards, they lay close, spent and content. They slept.

After what seemed but minutes, Jason awakened, chilled. Only faint embers glowed weakly in the fire pit. He crawled from the bed, added pieces of wood to the fire, blew on the embers to ignite the new fuel.

His head came up. He heard the clicking of the bare tree limbs whipping in the cold wind, but there was something else. There it was again, a brushing or snuffling. He reached under his saddle and clutched the pistol. Crawling to the opening, he looked outside.

The bright moonlight outlined a huge bear standing on all fours under the deer carcass, looking up.

The bear watched the carcass sway and revolve in the wind. Jason's jaw hung. He had seen black bears in Kentucky. This giant was no black bear. It was a golden brown monster, four times the size of any bear he had seen at home. This was a grizzly, larger than the one he had seen on the Stockton-bound steamer.

The bear watched the swaying carcass, his head moving in rhythm. Jason started when the bear stood on its hind legs and swatted at the dangling legs of the deer. His huge paws missed the deer's front legs by inches.

Jason was shocked. The bear would have dwarfed a man standing alongside. The grizzly dropped to all fours, still looking up at the carcass.

Jason's mind raced. He looked at the pistol he held. It felt like a stick of firewood. He thought of going for his rifle, but recalled the stories told in the Outpost that grizzlies, though shot a number of times by high-powered rifles, often charged the shooters before dying. He glanced sharply at the sleeping Tah-nee.

The bear lifted again on his hind legs below the carcass. Jayson reached through the u-ma-cha opening and aimed the pistol. He fired. The bark on the tree trunk over the bear's shoulder exploded, showering splinters. The bear dropped heavily to all fours and swung around to face the source of the shot. He looked directly at Jason, his head swinging side to side. He roared, stepped toward the u-ma-cha.

Jason fired again, and again the bark on the trunk exploded. The bear stopped, his head swinging rapidly. Suddenly he whirled and ran down the hillside.

Jason leaned back, sat down heavily, the pistol in his lap. He inhaled deeply, exhaled. Only then did he see the rifle barrel over his shoulder. Tahnee lowered the rifle, sat beside him in the opening. She smiled.

"Whooo," he said.

"He big. Biggest I ever see. I think he not come back."

"I thought bears hibernated in winter. That monster didn't look sleepy."

"Sometime bear wake up early when he very hungry."

"I glad you not let bear get deer." She put a morsel of venison in her mouth and wiped her hands with a cloth.

"Yeah, me too. But I'm not taking any chances. I took it down and pulled it down the slope to the swale. If he's real hungry and remembers that deer and the two-legged that scared him off, he might decide to give us another try. I hope he'll be satisfied with the carcass down the hill and forget about us."

They sat quietly at the fire circle, staring into the flames, sipping coffee from tin cups. The wind had decreased at dusk, and a light snow fell, noiselessly. She added boughs to the fire, sat back, finished her coffee, watching the dancing flames.

"Do you see many grizzlies where you live?" he said.

"Not so many our home. We live in deep valley, see black bears our valley, grizzly in high mountains. But we know grizzly. Jay-son, I tell you story about grizzly, Ahwahneechee story. Okay?"

"Yes, I would like that. I want to know everything about your people."

She looked from the fire to the peak where the thin smoke spiral splintered and filtered through the gathered tops of poles. Closing her eyes, she opened them and looked into the flames.

"Long, long time ago, my people ancestors live in peace in Ah-wah-nee, my valley. One day young man go lake to spear fish. Before he reach lake, big grizzly step from behind rock and stand in middle of trail. Young man take limb from dead tree and fight bear. They fight long time. Young man hurt by teeth and claw of bear, but he finally kill bear. When he tell people about fight, they say he very brave. They honor him by naming him Yo-sem-i-te. This is name for full-grown grizzly. This name pass to his children and finally to whole tribe. We are Ahwahneechee, Yosemite."

"Good story," he said. "So you are a grizzly bear."

"Yes. You be good me, or I grab you, bite you." She smiled. "You want fight me?"

He stared at her, grim. Then: "Yes!" He lunged for her, and they rolled on the ground. She pushed on his chest, he grappled, his arms encircling her waist, she rolled and wriggled aside, finally pinned under his body, both panting. He lay on her, his face over hers.

"I have you, little grizzly," he said. He kissed her lightly.

"You win, brave warrior. You do what you want me."

# Chapter 10

Jason rode through a snow pack a foot deep, his horse making a crunching noise with each step on the crusty snow. His rifle was strapped on his back. A scarf wrapped around his neck and ears, his hat pulled down snugly. He rode to a wooded ridge almost bare of snow.

Topping the ridge, he reined in at the edge of timber. He looked down into a swale, a broad largely treeless corridor that was heavy with snow. On the near side, below the ridge where Jason sat his horse, three men huddled around a fire. Their horses were tied to saplings nearby.

Jason started to turn his horse back into cover when one of the men saw him. "Hey, up there!" The man's companions turned and saw him. Jason rode off the ridge down the slope toward the men.

He pulled up beside the fire and dismounted.

"What in hell you doin' up here middle of winter," said the one who had spotted him.

Jason tied his horse to a sapling beside the others. "Hunting," he said. He pulled the rifle from his shoulder and leaned it against the trunk of the sapling, squatted at the fire and warmed his hands. "Game is pretty well gone near my claim. Also thought I would look around for some likely feeder streams to work come spring. Didn't count on the snow. This is my first winter in the country."

"Well, you ain't too smart, that's for sure." The man smiled. "Come to that, we ain't either. We thought we could shoot meat on this ride—but you're right about that—not much game about. We only shot two squirrels, fat little critters, but thin fare for three growed men. Sorry we can't offer you anything." The men hardly paused their repast as they talked, pulling strips of flesh from the two carcasses that had been skewered and roasted over the fire.

"This fire is all I need right now. I was getting mighty cold up there," Jason said, his hands still held before the fire. "What're you boys doing up here? You're surely not thinking of trying to cross the mountains."

"Hell no, we ain't that dumb. We're looking for signs of a thaw. It's gettin' plain balmy in Mariposa, but don't see no sign of spring up here."

"Mariposa. Are you with the volunteer group that Mr. Savage is putting together?"

"Yep, we are the advance guard," said another.

The third man frowned. "We're *what?* 'Advance guard'?"

"The advance guard, the brave who go before and make the way safe," said the first speaker.

"Kelly, you're so fulla horse doo-doo that I don't understand you half the time."

Kelly extended his hand to Jason. "I'm Kelly, that's L.J. over there with his mouth full of squirrel meat, and the third member of the advance guard is Jeremy." Jeremy, of the horse doo-doo comment, ducked his head, smiled. L.J. waved a quick, brushing-a-fly wave, his mouth full of squirrel meat.

"In answer to your question," said Kelly, "yes, we are part of Mr. Savage's volunteer group. He sent us up here on this wild good chase. From the looks of things, spring ain't comin' around here till summer. I expect the battalion will rest in Mariposa some time longer."

"It might be just as well," said L.J., wiping his hands on his trousers. "Mr. Savage said he might have to go over to San Jose to talk with some federal people who plan to make up treaties with the Indians to move them to the Fresno reservation. He said he expects there's gonna be people there who will take the side of the Indians. He said most everbody at that gathering won't have no idea what's goin' on, especially the federal people, and he'll have to set 'em straight."

Jason frowned, staring into the fire. "The federal people are in San Jose now? Why San Jose?"

"San Jose's the new state capital. Did you know California's a state now?" said L.J.

"Actually, I didn't," said Jason. "You said there will be people at this meeting taking the side of the Indians?"

"Yeah," said Kelly, "some people who claim that Indians have rights to the land where they live and should either keep the land or be paid to leave it. The federal people plan to deal with the question in the treaties. Mr. Savage wants to be sure that the treaties will force the Indians to move to the Fresno River reservation. He was a friend to the Indians till they started shooting up his own trading posts. Now he believes there's no way to get all this settled without making the Indians move to reservations in the valley."

Kelly stood. "Now we've wasted enough time here. We need to git home and tell Mr. Savage that he has plenty of time to go to San Jose. The battalion ain't riding into the mountains any time soon."

L.J. and Jeremy and Jason stood, and all went to their horses.

"You're welcome to ride down with us if you're finished gallivantin' around in the snow," said Kelly.

"Thanks for the offer," Jason said, "but I need to collect the gear at my camp and get back to the claim. Don't see anything promising up here. Didn't find any game either. Seems you got all of the squirrels." He smiled.

The three men mounted. "Take care of yourself, pard," said L.J. "There's hostiles about." They moved off, riding in the path they had beaten down that morning.

Jason watched them working their way down the trail, single file, until they disappeared around a stand of pines. He still stood, staring, pondering.

*Hostiles. Yes, there sure are hostiles about.*

Tahnee and Jason sat at the fire circle inside the u-ma-cha. The wind whispered in the bare branches and sent gusts of cold wind down the vent at the peak of the slanted poles. On his ride back up the hill, scattered small snowflakes whirled about the treetops. By the time he reached camp at dusk, the light fall had turned to heavy, wet snow.

"The battalion is not going to be able to move in this weather, and we probably can't either. I'm thinking I should go to San Jose and talk with the people there. Maybe if I added my support to those who believe that Indians have rights to their land, it could matter."

"I go too, talk about my people and my valley," she said.

"I don't think that would be a good idea. There will be some Indian-haters there, and you haven't been in your valley almost two years now. They might ask questions you can't answer. We don't even know where your people are, in the valley or somewhere else."

"What I do?"

"We'll put you up with Bess. I think she'll be glad to see you. Since Savage is going to be at San Jose, I can keep an eye on him and move out before he does. The battalion won't go anywhere until he returns to Mariposa. We'll leave here in the morning."

"We leave u-ma-cha just like this. Maybe use it again. Okay?"

He reached for her, pushed his hand inside her shirt. "Okay, my little brown sweetheart Miwok Yosemite princess. Now let's get to bed." He kissed her and caressed her breast.

She took his cheeks in both hands. "Okay, you silly white man 'merican miner."

She built up the fire, followed him to the bed and climbed in. The fire burned brightly, crackling, tongues of flames rising and swaying, the storm howling in the bare black treetops, their love-making a reflection and part of their violent surroundings.

Afterwards, he held her tightly, then released her and rolled on his back, exhaling deeply. He turned on his side toward her. She put a hand to his cheek, kissed him lightly. He took the hand, kissed it.

"Tell me a Miwok story," he said.

She sat up, leaned over and placed some boughs on the fire. The dry wood caught, and flames leapt from the embers. She leaned back, pulled the blanket over her crossed legs, stared through the opening of the u-ma-cha into the darkness, the flames casting dancing slivers of light on the fresh snow. She pulled the blanket up around her shoulders.

"Okay. A woman name Tis-se-yak and her husband travel to country far away. When they came back Ah-wah-nee, they very tired, very thirsty. They hurry to lake to drink. She reach lake first, she so thirsty she drink all water in lake. This very bad for valley. All grass and trees die.

"Husband very angry, he so thirsty. He beat his wife with big stick. She run away, but he catch her and beat her more. She cry, then become very angry and throw basket at him. Then something happen. Because they both so bad, they turn to stone, husband with basket beside him and woman's stone face marked with long lines, her tears.

"This true story. I show you stone man and woman in valley."

He looked up at her. "Hmm."

"You don't believe?"

"It's a good story. I like it."

"You don't believe. You believe stories 'bout Christian God? Linda tell me about white man God."

"Um, yes, I believe."

"You believe God make woman from bone of man? You believe Jesus turn water to wine?"

"Uh, Tahnee, you're going to make my head hurt."

"You be careful, you turn stone!" She lay down, leaned over and kissed him lightly, closed her eyes and snuggled.

"You think you can put up with us a few days, Bess?" Jason and Tahnee stood at the open door of Billy's Rooms.

"Lordy," said Bess, "I'm glad to see you again. I missed you. Didn't 'spect to see you so soon. We sure can put up with you, as long as you can put up with us." She stepped aside. "Come on in. Put your stuff in your room, the same one, and I'll put on some coffee. Billy'll be glad to see you."

Jason and Tahnee unloaded the packs from the mule, carried them inside and stacked them in a corner of their room. He left Tahnee in the dining room and went out to take the animals to the livery.

Jason returned in a half hour and joined Tahnee and Bess in the dining room. Bess poured him a coffee, and everyone sat.

"I expect I'll be gone at least a week, maybe longer. Two weeks? Don't know how long this will take, the riding and the talking. I'll have to ask around. Billy said that Savage and a couple of others left for San Jose just yesterday. I'm leaving tomorrow morning, so I could run into them on the road. I haven't decided whether that would be a good idea.

"I'll be real interested in hearing Savage tell how his friendship with the Indians changed. I suppose he was friendly as long as he could control them, as long as they would trade with him on his conditions. I understand he didn't get too agitated when Indians attacked some miners and trading posts owned by other people. All that changed when they started attacking *his* trading posts. Now he wants all of the mountain Indians to move to the reservation, the peaceful Indians by choice and the hostiles by force."

"Are you going to be in any danger?" Bess looked from Jason to Tahnee. "Sorry, missy." She patted Tahnee's hand on the table.

"Nah, I hear the valley's peaceful and almost clear of snow. The only problems around here seem to be where white men are pushing Indians off their lands. That's what I intend to talk about at San Jose."

He stood. “I’m going to get my stuff together. I told Billy I want to make an early start.”

Jason stood with Tahnee and Bess on the sidewalk in front of the house. Billy held the reins of Jason’s horse. A pair of filled saddlebags was strapped behind the saddle.

“I hate to lay this on you folks, but I’m trusting you to take care of this one and not let her get herself in any trouble.” He smiled.

“Don’t you worry,” said Bess. “She’s my little sister, and I’ll keep her in line and in sight.”

“I know you will. I wouldn’t trust anybody else with her.” He put both hands on Tahnee’s cheeks and kissed her lightly. “You mind Bess and stay close, hear?”

“Go on, big grizzly. I take care myself.” She hooked an arm around Bess’s arm. “You take care you self.”

Jason stepped off the sidewalk, took the reins from Billy who clapped him on the back. Jason mounted and rode away at a lope. He waved over his shoulder.

Jason rode through a land just awakening from winter. Mountain ranges, clearly visible on cloudless days, running south to north, bordered the broad valley on the east and west. Though snow still lay on the land, some trees displayed early leaf buds, and birds filled the air with their song. He met travelers from time to time who varied from morose and rude to open and friendly. He passed some hours with the latter, riding and sharing an evening campfire. He began to think that California might be worth considering as home.

Riding into San Jose, Jason found a hodgepodge of old and new. San Jose's selection as the first capital of the new state of California had stimulated an influx of newcomers and new construction. The old Spanish-Mexican pueblo was fast becoming an American town.

He wondered how he was going to learn where the federal commissioners and state officials were holding discussions. Remembering that he learned all he needed to know about Mariposa at the Hideout, he asked on the streets about a similar institution and found the saloon owned by State Senator Thomas Jefferson Green. When he went inside, he saw a well-dressed gentleman leaning on the bar, sipping his whiskey. A ring of similarly dressed men crowded around him, drinks in hand, leaning in, grinning, listening intently. Jason learned soon enough that the dandy at the center of attention was Green himself.

Gradually, Jason inserted himself into the group. Learning of Jason's interest, Green invited him to come to the nearby hall the next day where the Indian question indeed was being discussed. Jason thanked him, asked for a recommendation for lodging, and was directed to a boarding house down the street. Also owned by Senator Thomas Jefferson Green.

Next morning, Jason entered the hall where two dozen men sat, stood and milled about, waiting. He saw Senator Green speaking to a knot of men who listened and laughed often. Though Jason wore his best, he and a couple of others appeared out of place among the well-dressed, well-groomed assemblage.

All turned toward the door when a quartet of men strode in, deep in conversation. The room fell silent as the four took seats behind a table facing the room. Others in the room found seats among the chairs arrayed in rows before the table. Jason sat in the last row on an outside aisle.

One of the men at the table stood. "Gentlemen. Thus far, we have talked about the Indian problem. Today we need to talk about a solution to the Indian problem. For those who have not been with us before today, I should introduce our three commissioners from Washington, here to negotiate treaties with the Indians." He gestured to the men at the table with him. "Matthew Johnson, Abel Maples and Hiram Edwards. I am Senator Jonathan Montague.

"Let me just review where we are in the discussion. State officials have spoken out about the Indian problem. Both Governor Burnett and Governor McDougal, who took office last January, would have the Indian problem solved by exterminating the Indians. The three federal commissioners decided that was extreme and unwise and have tried to negotiate with tribes to relocate them to areas that were not occupied or desired by white men. That policy proved impractical. The commissioners have since accepted a proposal by Edward F. Beale, the California Indian Superintendent, to remove the mountain Indians to reservations in the valley. That is the policy that we intend to implement. Questions?" He sat down.

Members of the audience looked around, expectantly, but no one spoke. They looked back to the front.

Senator Montague stood, looked around. "Since there are no questions—"

"Sir." Jason stood in the aisle beside his chair. "May I ask a question?"

"You may indeed. And you are, sir?"

"Jason Bishop, sir, miner, lately of Kentucky." Jason waited for a response, but Montague simply stared.

"I'm wondering," said Jason, "since the Indians were living in their villages in the mountains long before the whites arrived, don't they own their land? Don't they have rights to where they live?"

The room was suddenly silent as everyone turned to look at Jason. He ignored the stares, awaiting Montague's response. When Jason said no more, they looked back to the front at Montague and the three commissioners, who looked at each other, as if to ask, how does one reply to this simpleton?

Montague frowned. He spoke slowly, as one explains a complicated premise to a child or one who is not expected to understand. "I think you were not here yesterday. We touched on that point. Raiding and killing are an integral part of the natives' culture. This behavior cannot be tolerated in a civilized country." He sat down, signaling an end to the exchange.

"But weren't the Indians responding to the whites' killing off the game, cutting down their acorn trees and encroaching on the land they had lived on for generations, long before the white men came?"

Montague stared at the tabletop, noticeably annoyed. He looked up. "Are you suggesting that the savages have a right to the land?"

"Yes, sir. I am saying that." Jason was warming to the discussion. He shifted his feet, stiffened. "If they have raided and killed, wasn't that in response to the whites burning their villages and killing them when they resisted?"

Montague looked sternly at Jason. He leaned on his fists on the table. "By God, sir, you go too far! I would have you—"

"Gentlemen! Gentlemen!" Everyone turned to see Senator Green standing at the front, smiling, facing the audience. "This splendid debate has made me increasingly thirsty! Let's adjourn to my establishment for refreshment. The first drink's on the house, and the second drink is double price."

The tension broke as all laughed and agreed that this was an excellent idea. Amidst back-slapping and laughs and chatter, all headed for the door. All but one man who stood at his chair, front row, right side, glowering at Jason.

It was James Savage. In his nervousness and the heated debate, Jason had forgotten about him.

In Mariposa, Jason had managed to avoid Savage's notice. That would no longer be possible.

When Jason returned to the hearing room the next morning, a guard at the door prevented him from entering. This is a closed meeting, the guard told him.

# Chapter 11

Jason rode with his head hanging, pondering. He wondered whether he had made a point that the authorities would consider. Or had his effort hardened their resolve against any opinion other than their own? The only sure result of his speaking out at the meeting was that Savage now knew him.

The weather had turned ugly, matching his mood. A light rain on his departure from San Jose turned to snow flurries that would make the remainder of his ride to Mariposa miserable. He hunched his shoulders and pulled the collar of his coat up. He urged his horse into a lope.

Jason tied the reins of his horse at the post outside Billy's Rooms. He looked overhead. The light rain and snow that morning had ended by noon, but the low gray ceiling promised more weather. The orange sun ball lay in a saddle in the dark mountain range westward across the valley.

Shivering, he untied the bags from behind the saddle and went to the door. He knocked and waited. The door opened, and there stood Bess with a glum expression. His smile turned to a frown. He had never seen this face. She stepped back for him to enter, closed the door behind him and started down the hall.

"Bess," he said, "what is it?"

She stopped, turned around. "You need to talk to Tahnee. She's in your room. She won't come out except for meals. Been waiting for you."

He strode down the hall, opened the door, and saw Tahnee sitting at the window, staring outside. She looked up, stood and came to him. He dropped the saddlebags and encircled her shoulders, drew her to him. She held him tightly around his waist.

He pulled back, took her head in his hands, raised her face. "What's wrong?"

She took him by a hand and led him to the dining room door where Bess waited. "Bess, can we have coffee?" Tahnee said. "You too." Bess nodded and walked to the kitchen.

Jason and Tahnee sat at their usual place at the window. They were alone in the room. His hands were on the table, and she took his hands in hers.

"You cold," she said.

"I'm okay. First time I've been warm since leaving San Jose. Tahnee, what—"

"Wait for Bess. Please. . . . You have good meeting San Jose?"

"Well, I made my case, talked about the rights of Indians and said that when they fought back, they were just trying to defend themselves and their villages and land."

She tried to smile, looked down at their hands. She pulled her hands back and put them in her lap, glanced absentmindedly through the window. The morning rain had turned to a mist that lifted just before he arrived. The cold lingered under the gray overcast.

Bess brought in a tray holding three filled coffee cups. She set the tray in the middle of the table. Each took a cup, and she sat in the chair between Jason and Tahnee.

Tahnee sipped from her cup as the others watched her. She set the cup down, looked up at Jason. "You remember man grab me at Hideout?"

"Yes," said Jason.

"He catch me on sidewalk when—"

"Tahnee, I told you not to go out except with Bess or Billy."

"Hang on, Jason, she was with me," said Bess.

"Then how—"

"She wanted to stay on the sidewalk when I went in the store. Poor girl had not been outside the house in days. I was going to be in the store only a few minutes. I'm sorry. Didn't think anything could go wrong in a few minutes."

"I'll kill him!" Jason said.

Tahnee took his hand. "Jay-son, he say he have gun under coat. He say he shoot me if I not go with him. He take me storeroom behind Hideout. He say take off clothes and be quiet, or I shoot. He crazy! I not know what to do. Just then Bess come through door. She yell 'you sumbitch,' and he jump for her. She pick up hammer and hit him on head. He stumble back, drop knife. I get knife from floor. He come for me . . ." She put her hands to her head. "Jay-son, he grab me, I stick him in stomach, he grab my neck, I stick him again. He fall back against wall and fall on floor."

Jason looked from Tahnee to Bess and back at Tahnee. He waited.

"I took it from there, Jason," Bess said. "I checked him, and he was dead, for sure. Now this town ain't too friendly to Indians. You know that. I looked outside and didn't see nobody. People don't much go out behind the stores on that side of the road. We dragged him across that little dry streambed and up the other side to a bunch of downed stuff. We dug a hole with a shovel I got from the storeroom and pulled him in. We shoveled the dirt in and covered everything with leaves and brush and rocks. He ain't gonna be found. I put the shovel back in the store-room, closed the door. We went back to my place, and Tahnee had her first whiskey."

Tahnee had listened to Bess without taking her eyes from Jason. She held his hand tightly. "I sorry, Jay-son."

"How did you know, Bess?" Jason said.

"When I come out of the store and saw her gone, I asked a couple of people on the sidewalk. One woman said she saw her walking between the two stores toward the back with a man. She said she didn't think anything of it. People around here don't think too much about what happens to Indians, you know. Me, when it was all over, I felt like cuttin' the sumbitch into little pieces. It was Tahnee who came up with the idea of burying him. . . . Jason, I hope we did right."

"Right?" He grinned, leaned over to Bess, kissed her on the cheek. "My, my, you two are something. I would have killed him and got in big trouble. You did it right. My two angels. The only thing bad about this is that we need to pack up and move out. That ya-hoo's pard might be glad to be rid of him, or he might be looking for him right now. If he talks with the same woman you talked to, Bess, we're in trouble."

He looked through the window to the dark yard. "If we had any sense, we'd leave right now, but I don't think anything's likely to happen tonight. We need to be gone at first light. Bess, would you tell Billy?" She nodded.

Jason and Tahnee watched Bess collect the coffee cups and walk toward the hall. "Thanks, Bess," said Jason. She stopped, looked back, smiled and went out.

"You sure everything okay?" Tahnee said. "I was just so, so *angry*. Why do white men do that, why they think they can do anything they want? You the only white man who treat me like a person. You and Billy. Other white men think I just a toy, something to play with. Why they do that?"

He stood, bent and kissed her forehead. "No man has the right to even touch you if you don't welcome the touch. And if you don't welcome it, I'm going to beat hell out of that man. That is, I will if you haven't already stuck him." She smiled, squeezed his hand.

He walked to the stove, extended his hands over the top.

"You cold?" she said.

He looked at her over his shoulder. "You don't like cold hands."

She stood and went to him, took his arm and led him down the hall to their room. Inside, they shed clothes quickly in the cold room and climbed into bed, pulled up covers. He touched her breast under the blanket.

"Warm," she said.

He pulled the cover down to expose the breast. He kissed the nipple, bit gently.

"Ai! You bite!" She hit him lightly on the chest.

"Shush. Bess will come in to see if you are all right."

He caressed the breast, kissed her lips. "I missed you, my little Yosemite sweetheart."

She turned on her side, kissed him. "Jay-son, you remember what 'Yosemite' mean?"

He frowned. "It means a bunch of troublesome Indians."

"No. Remember I said it mean 'grownup grizzly?' Remember I can take care myself. Maybe take care you too." She smiled.

He frowned. "Okay, my little grownup she-grizzly, this warrior grizzly is going to wrestle you!"

"I no want wrestle. I want do sex."

"Hah!" He laughed out loud.

"Shh. Bess come."

With help from Billy and Bess, Jason and Tahnee left town the next morning at dawn. Billy had the horses and mule out front when they came out with Bess. They loaded the mule with the tent and blankets Billy had bought for them and tied saddlebags behind saddles. Tahnee hugged Bess, they mounted and waved goodbye.

They duplicated the route they had taken the last time they left Mariposa. Riding out on the Stockton trail, they turned north when the town was a shadow at the foot of the mountains, then turned eastward.

The rolling plain of the eastern central valley was still a white landscape, but the thaw had begun, and occasional snow flurries did not add to the thin pack. It all changed when they rode from the plain into the foothills, which seemed still to be gripped by winter. The horses and mule plowed through deep snow, and a light snowfall was almost constant.

As they rode up the wooded slope and neared the u-ma-cha, Tahnee reined to a stop and held out a hand to stop Jason.

He pulled up, leaned over and spoke softly. "What—"

She shook her head, staring at the u-ma-cha. They sat silent, still. Suddenly a gray fox darted from the u-ma-cha opening and ran for cover up the slope. The rusty red color of the neck and ears flashed against the gray of his coat.

Tahnee turned to Jason, smiling. "It dark inside u-ma-cha, but I see nose in opening."

They reined up in front of the u-ma-cha. It was intact but for a couple of gaping holes in the siding where slabs of bark had blown away. Tahnee mended the covering while Jason unloaded the mule and led the animals to the pen above camp. He hobbled them and gave them some barley. The rivulet near camp was running, and he scooped water in a bucket for the animals.

By the time he reached the u-ma-cha, the light snow had turned heavy, and the temperature was dropping. He stooped and went inside. It was glorious to be out of the wind and almost warm. Tahnee had collected wood and built a fire. The coffee pot was just beginning to steam. He squatted beside the fire and sat down heavily, exhaled.

"Whew. I'm tired. Let's eat from the pack to-night, and I'll shoot some meat tomorrow. That okay?"

"Okay. Full-grown grizzly eat anything." She fixed a simple meal of jerked beef, hardtack and dried apples, washed down by strong coffee. When they were finished, they built up the fire and crawled into bed, bone tired. Both were asleep in minutes.

By early afternoon the next day, the snowfall had ended, but the temperature had lowered. Jason decid-ed that it was too late in the day to hunt. He would ride down the slope to look at the trail and check the snow pack. He said he would hunt tomorrow, if the snow were not too deep. They would need meat since it appeared they might be in this camp a few days yet before attempting to ride to Tahnee's valley.

He looked down at her, sitting at the fire circle, chewing a hardtack wafer. She placed a couple of sticks on the embers, leaned back and watched the dancing flames. He stared, motionless. *I love this woman. Is that possible?*

She looked up. "What?"

He smiled, his reverie broken. "I loaded the rifle, and you know where the balls, caps and powder are. I expect you'll have no need of it, but it's there in case a fat doe walks into the yard. I'll be back before dark."

He loaded the Colt and pushed it into its holster. Hefting his saddle, he bent and carried it through the u-ma-cha opening.

She followed him outside, reached for him and pulled his head down, kissed him. "Be careful . . . sweetheart." She ducked her head, laughed. He bent, kissed the top of her head and lightly bit her ear.

"Ouch!" She jerked away and swatted his arm. "Don't do that!" She rubbed her ear.

He laughed. Dropping the saddle, he took her cheeks in both hands, kissed her on the mouth, pulled back and looked into her eyes. She put her hands on his, pulled him down and kissed him.

He picked up the saddle and turned to go. "Now get to work." She swatted him on his arm as he danced away, laughing.

Walking to the animal pen, he saddled his horse and tended to the mule and Tahnee's mare. He mounted and rode past the u-ma-cha down the slope toward an aspen grove that marked the main trail from the valley to the high country.

He looked up. The weak sun was misleading. A lacy gray overcast foretold more weather. He continued down the slope, his horse stepping gingerly in the knee-high snow. He reined in under an overhanging sugar pine branch when he saw movement in a manzanita thicket at the base of a stand of Ponderosa pines. He waited.

A rider emerged from the manzanita, followed by three others. When Jason's horse nickered, the riders looked up the slope and saw him. The lead rider waved. Jason pondered, then rode down to the men.

"You still out hunting, are yuh?" said the lead rider. It was Kelly, the head of the advance guard that had confronted Jason in almost this same place. Jason glanced at the other three. He thought he recognized one of the men.

"Well, just looking right now," Jason said. "Not much game in this snow. I need—"

"Kelly, I know this man," said the fourth rider who had stared at Jason from the time he rode up. Jason remembered. This was Bonney, sidekick of the man that Jason had demolished after he had accosted Tahnee in front of the Hideout. "I thank he just might know what happened to Bart."

Kelly looked at Bonney, frowned. "What makes you think so? I thought Bart left town."

"Well, he mighta left town, but I bet he wasn't ridin' no horse when he left. Bart had his eye on a Indian woman, and this man thought she was his, and he and Bart had a set-to. Anyway, Bart didn't tell me he was leavin' town, and he woulda told me if he planned to leave. I don't know what happened to him."

"That right? Uh, Jason, ain't it?" said Kelly.

"Jason, yes. I haven't the foggiest idea what he's talking about. Yeah, I had a set-to with the man called Bart. I beat hell out of him. Not long after, I went to San Jose for a few days, came back for one night, then left. Ask Bess and Billy. Ask Mr. Savage about San Jose. He saw me there."

"It don't wash, Kelly," said Bonney. "The sheriff needs to have a look at this."

Kelly raised his chin, eyes closed, opened them and looked at Jason. He obviously wanted no part in this. "Well, Jason, since this Bart fella has disappeared, and you admit to whupping him, I suppose you better go back to Mariposa to explain all this to Sheriff Burney. He's a reasonable man and won't hold you if you can convince him that you know nothing about Bart's disappearance." He leaned over toward Jason. "I'll just take the pistol belt."

Jason unfastened the belt and handed it to Kelly. "My partners are going to worry about me. I hope they don't come to Mariposa looking for me. They can get a bit edgy."

Kelly smiled. "I suspect the Sheriff and people of Mariposa outnumber your partners. Besides, your partners will just figure you're hot on the trail of the biggest grizzly bear in the state of Californie.

"Okay, you boys better be on your way. Eddie, you're in charge. Bonney, you go so you can tell the sheriff your side of the story." Kelly pointed at Bonney. "If I hear that you laid a hand on Jason on the way down, I'll make you wish you was never born."

Bonney smirked. "Whatever you say, boss."

"Me and Fred will move up this trail one more day," said Kelly. "I expect to find too much snow to give any encouragement to Mr. Savage, so we'll be down dreckly."

Bonney and the other man took up position on each side of Jason, and the three set off down the slope.

"I don't rightly know what to make of this." The speaker was Sheriff Burney. He stood with Bonney and the other rider on the sidewalk in front of his office. "The fact that he beat the tar outta Bart don't mean he killed him.

"I've been talking to people ever since he was reported missing, but nobody knows anything. The only person who even saw him on the day he went missing was a woman who *thinks* she saw him walking with a woman toward the alley behind the Outpost. But that don't mean anything. It might *not* have been him. And Bart was well known to be woman-crazy. Maybe crazy all by itself. There's no report of a woman missing, so I don't know what to make of it.

"Course, I'll talk to Bess and Billy, like Jason said, and also Mr. Savage. I suspect they'll back up Jason's story. So I'm wondering whether I can justify feeding and housing him until the judge comes our way again."

"Sheriff, I saw him when he picked the fight with Bart," Bonney said. "I thought he was gonna kill him right then and there. Have you talked with the Indian woman? Teddy told me they wanted to stay at his place first time they come to Mariposa, and he sent them to Billy's. Maybe Billy knows something."

"I'll ask." Burney put a hand on each of the men's shoulder. "Okay, you boys done your job. Now you can cool your heels and wet your whistles. I'll look you up if I have any questions for you."

"What about Jason?"

"You're finished with Jason. He's my concern now. Go on."

Bonney's companion tugged at his sleeve. "C'mon. The sheriff had a good idea. I'm thirsty." Bonney frowned, hesitated, followed him, walking slowly on the plank sidewalk, head down.

The sheriff watched them go, then turned and went into his office. Jason sat in a chair beside the desk. Burney sat down in the chair behind the desk, leaned back. "Young Bart was a troublemaker the minute he set foot in this town. Drunk brawling, cussing at the church ladies, making a general nuisance of hisself. Anyway, I don't think you have anything to do with him missing, but I got my job to do, so I'll have to ask you to be my guest for a day or two while I do some checking around. This won't take long. I hope."

"Can I see Billy and Bess?"

"I'll tell 'em you'd like to talk, and they can come to the office." The sheriff stood. "Now, all this work has made me hungry. Since you're my prisoner, and I'm responsible for feeding you, and I haven't made any arrangements for meals, what do you say we go over to the café for some lunch? The people of Mariposa County are buying."

# Chapter 12

Sheriff Burney had pronounced lunch the most satisfying meal he had partaken in months, testifying to the fine cooking and the stimulating conversation. He apologized for having to return Jason to the cell at his office.

Now he sat with Bess in her dining room. The sheriff slumped in his chair at the window table. Both held coffee cups.

"He was with us, in this house, the whole time he was in town, from when he arrived till he left," Bess said. "Well, he went to the livery first to leave his horse with Billy. When him and Tahnee left, Billy had the horses waiting out front. There's no way he coulda done in your man unless he sneaked out in the middle of the night, and I woulda known. I'm a light sleeper. Anyway, the day you said your man disappeared, Jason was in San Jose."

"Yep, I confirmed that with Mr. Savage. He saw Jason in San Jose." Burney stood.

"You gonna let him go?"

"I don't see how I can keep him. I don't want to keep him. Seems like a nice fella. I'll be letting him go unless something turns up real soon." He took his hat from the back of the chair, put it on.

"Thanks for the coffee, Bess. Much appreciated." He followed her to the door and went out, touched his hat brim to her.

*****

"Sheriff, I won't say it's been a pleasure, but I appreciate the clean bed and the café meals. Now I'm going to have to go back up the mountain to scrounge for my meals and sleep on pine needles. I think I'm going to tell my pards that we need to spend time in Mariposa till spring thaw."

Jason and the sheriff stood on the walk in front of his office. Burney looked up at the clear sky.

"That might not be long off. Doesn't look like spring's coming just yet, but it does look like winter's just about ending. Last I heard, Major Savage is fixing to move out. Kelly come in yesterday and talked to him. He's put out the call for the volunteers to be ready to ride any time now."

Jason put on his hat and buttoned up his coat. "Then I'd best be on my way. I want to get back up the hill before that mob scares away all the game." He extended his hand. "Sheriff Joe Burney, you're a good man. When I see you again, I hope it's just to renew the acquaintance over a whiskey."

Burney smiled, gripped the hand and shook it. "Take care of yourself. Stay out of sight of the battalion. A lot of the volunteers are just young boys hoping for some excitement. Some of 'em will be looking for a chance to shoot somebody. As for shooting, hang on." He stepped into his office, came back with Jason's pistol and belt. He handed it to him. "Expect you'd like to have this back. It's not loaded. The boys said you was hunting or scouting about for game when they found you. Don't expect you'll have much luck with the Colt."

Jason laughed. "No, I'm not that good. I use an almost-new Leman, has a bit more range than the Colt. Bought it in San Francisco. The owner apparently had fancied himself a carver, but mercifully ended his attempt to carve an image of the head of a fork horn buck before disfiguring the stock altogether. The action and barrel were untouched. Good rifle. "

"It is indeed. Got one myself. Good deer gun. Now, you'll want to be on your way."

"Yep, I do. Thanks for the hospitality." Jason touched his hat to Burney and stepped into the street. He walked with head down, his mind racing.

*What has Tahnee been doing these five or six days since I left her? Since I was arrested! Will she still be there, in the u-ma-cha? Will she think I have abandoned her? God, how I miss her! . . . Jessie, is it okay? I can't be alone, Jessie. When I'm alone, I think too much. If I'm alone, I'm afraid I'll kill myself. If she's not there . . .*

"Hey!" He had bumped into a man who was crossing in front of him.

"Sorry," Jason mumbled, and went on.

Passing the feed store, he turned into the alley, walked to the livery. Billy looked up from the horse he was brushing.

"Sheriff finally git tired of your company?" Billy said.

"Yep. He booted me out. Now I've got to fend for myself. Billy, I'm going to the store for a few things, then up to your place for my stuff. If you can have the horse ready when I come back, I'll be on my way."

"He'll be ready to go and ready for a little run, I 'spect. Jason, I sold the last of your dust. Got a pretty good price. I waited until I heard that not much dust was coming in, the boys being all busy with the battalion. Bess will give you the money."

"Thanks, Billy. Appreciate that."

Jason walked to the house, and Bess opened the door to his knock.

She frowned. "Well, you don't look none the worse for being in a jailhouse."

"The sheriff runs a comfortable jail. He should charge for room and board. He's a good man."

"Yes, he is. I suppose you are on your way out?"

"I am, anxious to see whether Tahnee is still there or give up on waiting."

"She'll be there. I'm sure of it. Come in. I have something for you." Jason went in, and Bess closed the door. She walked into the kitchen and came out carrying a small leather pouch. "Billy said to give you this."

"Thanks, Bess." He opened the pouch and poured the coins into his palm. The gold pieces were mostly $5 half eagles, some quarter eagles, and a fistful of $1 coins. He looked at the latter, front and side. "Never seen this coin. Hmm. $1. That should be useful."

"Billy thought you might like 'em. The man he sold the dust to told him that he just got the $1 pieces. They're new."

"On the same subject. Bess, I'm going to ask a favor." He pulled his coat off. "This coat is my traveling bank. Feel this." He showed her the collar of the coat. She felt the coins in the collar, frowned. "And this." He held out the lapel. She felt more coins.

"What's this?"

"This was Jessie's work. She was afraid we might be robbed. These are large denomination gold coins, mostly $10 and $5 pieces. I won't need them while we are in the mountains. Would you keep them for me? I'll fetch them when I can use them. If I don't come for them in, say, five years, you'll find a good use for them."

"Don't be a silly man. Course, I'll keep 'em for you, and you'll be coming for them. And bring your little Tahnee with you next time. I like her. Now, you go get your horse. I'll have the coins out and have this stitched up when you get back. We'll have a cup of coffee before I send you on your way. Tahnee'll be glad to see you."

Jason walked to the livery and, while Billy was saddling his horse, he went out back. Snow still clung to the boughs of pines, but bare oak branches showed tiny green leaf buds. Billy brought the saddled horse out, and he walked back to the house with Jason, leading the horse.

Bess stood on the walk. She handed him the coat. "Bit lighter that it was, but just as warm, I bet," she said. "And here's the bag of things you asked me to buy, and a strap to tie it to your saddle horn."

Jason put on the coat, took the bag. "I'll miss you two," he said. "You've been like family to a couple of strangers who are trying to find their way. We won't forget it."

Jason tied the bag to the horn, put a foot in the stirrup and swung a leg up, then stopped before settling in the saddle. He was looking across the street. Bonney leaned against a store front, staring at the three. Jason got down, handed the reins to Billy. He walked slowly across the street, stopped in front of Bonney.

"Don't say anything, punk. Just listen. If I hear that any harm has come to Billy or Bess or their house or anything or anybody around them, I will find you and kill you twenty different ways. Do you understand me?"

Bonney smirked. "You ain't gonna be around, are you?"

Jason grabbed him under his chin and squeezed. Bonney gagged, his eyes bulging. Jason leaned in until he was nose-to-nose, spoke softly.

"Now you listen to me, you son of a bitch, if you so much as frown at my friends, I'll soon know about it, and you'll be a dead man. I'll visit the sheriff before leaving town to tell him about our conversation." He released Bonney, turned around and walked back to his horse. Bonney walked away, rubbing his neck.

"I'm riding to Burney's office on my way out," Jason said. "Let him know if you even suspect any problem." He shook Billy's hand, touched his hat to Bess and mounted.

Jason sat his horse on the slope below the u-ma-cha. He saw no movement, heard no sounds but the rustle of dry leaves and soft clicking of bare black tree limbs in the light breeze. Nothing seemed changed but the dusting of new snow that morning. He hugged his horse gently with his legs and moved slowly forward.

He pulled up before the u-ma-cha, looked around. It was too quiet, too still. Drawing the Colt, he dismounted slowly, looking around, searching. He tied the reins to a limb, walked to the u-ma-cha opening, bent and looked inside. He withdrew and walked around the u-ma-cha to the animal pen. The hobbled mule stood alone.

He strode to the u-ma-cha, stooped and went inside. The interior was warmer than outside, and a few embers in the fire pit still glowed. Tahnee's saddle was gone, and the Leman. He grabbed a bag, ran back to the animal pen. He gave the mule some barley, picked up the bucket and filled it at the rivulet, set it in the pen.

Running to his horse, he untied the reins with shaking hands. He stood stock still, staring at the saddle. *Where are you, Tahnee?*

He walked to the u-ma-cha entrance, leading the horse. He studied the footprints in the fresh snow. Between the u-ma-cha and the animal pen, there were prints on prints, and he could not make out how many people made them. Moving beyond the animal pen, he saw clearly the prints of three horses side-by-side.

He mounted and slowly followed the tracks. After a mile on what appeared to be a game trail, the prints disappeared on a stone surface that was bare of snow. Stopping, he searched the flat. Nothing. Then he noticed that snow still lay in the pine forest ahead. He rode along the edge of timber and finally found the prints leading into the forest on a game trail.

In this dense stand, the riders had lined out in single file, and the tracks on tracks made it impossible to know how many horses were leaving prints. He guessed that the tracks were from the same three horses.

Seeing horse droppings in the trail, he reined in and dismounted. He knelt, picked up one of the road apples, broke it open and felt the inside. Still the slightest hint of warmth. He mounted and moved out at a fast walk.

Each time the forest opened, he pushed the horse into a lope, then slowed to a walk when he entered timber again. They would not be far ahead, and he wanted to see them before they saw him. He needed to be close since he had only the pistol. They had at least one rifle. And Tahnee.

The trail ran unmistakably, gradually, lower in elevation. The thin snow cover had turned to mush in some places, but the tracks were still distinguishable except when the wet soil became firm, hard-packed sod or stone. Jason leaned to the side on his horse, searching the trail and the forest ahead.

Emerging from a dense stand of pine, the trail opened and dropped down a slope toward a wooded canyon. Jason reined in so hard his horse backed a few steps.

There they were, riding through low brush, only their shoulders and heads visible. Tahnee rode between the two men. The heads bobbed and swayed side to side as their mounts found their way down the steep, rocky trail.

Jason reined his horse into the cover of a stand of pines beside the trail. He looked toward the horizon. The sun lay just above the top of the forest canopy. They would be stopping soon. He would bide his time.

At dusk, Jason leaned against a small boulder, looking down on the rough camp. Blankets and bags were scattered on the ground near a small fire. Tahnee's horse and two others, still saddled, were tied to tree limbs nearby. Jason saw the Leman in its scabbard on a horse, not Tahnee's.

One man sat cross-legged at the fire, chewing on something, staring at the flames. The other, wearing a grimy broad-brimmed felt hat, sat on a log beside the fire, rolling a cigarette. He grinned at Tahnee who sat on the ground at the fire, her legs bound at the ankles.

Jason crept slowly, quietly, from boulder to boulder, gradually moving down the slope toward the camp.

The hat finished rolling the cigarette, picked up a burning stick from the fire and lit it. He said something to his pard, and both laughed. Tahnee turned away. The man at the fire lifted a bottle, took a long swallow. Without taking his eyes from Tahnee, he passed the bottle to the hat who took it, raised it and finished the bottle. The hat grimaced, shook his head and tossed the bottle into the brush. He laughed, said something and pointed at Tahnee. The other man smirked, said something.

The hat stood, snarled. The only word Jason understood was "mine."

"Hey, there's enough for both of us," the other said loudly.

The hat inhaled deeply, blew out smoke, tossed the cigarette in the fire. "Sure, if there's anything left when I finish." He grinned, walked a few steps to stand beside Tahnee. He leaned over her, reached down, grasped her shirt at the collar and jerked roughly, opening the shirt and exposing a breast.

"Oh, my, my, my, lookee what I got," said the hat. He bent down, put his hands under armpits and lifted her. She stood unsteadily on her bound feet, shuffled awkwardly aside.

Jason stepped from behind the boulder. "That'll do it." The Colt was aimed at the hat. "Move and you're a dead man."

The hat grabbed Tahnee and pulled her in front of him, his arm around her neck. "We'll see who's about to be dead." He snatched a knife from a belt sheath, held it at Tahnee's throat. "Mick, get that rifle." The man at the fire jumped up.

"Mick, you stay where you are," said Jason, the Colt still leveled on the hat, "and you might get out of this alive." Mick did not leave his spot at the fire.

"So what's it gonna be, cowboy," said the hat, "do I cut this one, or do you turn around and mind your own business?"

Suddenly Tahnee reached over her shoulder and raked the hat's face with her fingernails. He recoiled, both arms falling away, thrusting a hand to his cheek, blood oozing between his fingers, Tahnee rolling aside.

Jason fired. The hat's head exploded, and he fell sideways into a manzanita. Jason swung on Mick.

Mick threw his hands in the air. "Don't shoot! I had nothin' to do with this. I was just watching."

"Go find your horse."

Mick stood and turned his back on Jason, walked toward the horses. He glanced over his shoulder, saw Jason look at Tahnee. Mick whipped around, pistol drawn and coming up. Before he could bring it up, Jason fired, striking him in the chest and blowing him backward. He took two stumbling steps and collapsed on his back, arms outstretched, still gripping the pistol. At the shot, the horses' heads jerked back sharply. The reins of two horses snapped, and the horses bolted, galloping into the dark forest.

Jason stared at the body that had been Mick. The split-second after he told Mick to find his horse, he thought: then what will I do with him? Mick solved that problem when he tried to pull down on Jason.

Jason shook his head, walked to the fire circle, nudged the two bodies with a foot. Pushing his pistol into the holster, he walked to Tahnee.

She grabbed him around his waist, held him tightly, her head buried in the folds of his coat. She shuddered. He put a hand on the back of her head, stroked her hair. Leaning down, he rested his cheek on her head.

"Okay?" he said.

She pulled away, exhaled. "Okay."

He helped her hobble to the log and sit down. Untying the rope, he tossed it in the fire. He took her cheeks in his hands, kissed her. "You're a lot of trouble, you know."

"Me! Where you been? I thought you just ride down the hill."

He winced. "That's it? Tahnee, I've been gone a week. You weren't worried?"

"You gone five days. You big boy, you can take care youself. I no worry."

"I was worried sick! I was afraid you would decide I was dead. Or run off."

"You big boy. You decide what you want do."

He shook his head, wrapped his arms around her and held her. "Well, I was worried. I wasn't sure you would still be here."

She took his face in her hands. "I know you, how you think. I think you not leave me unless you tell me."

He smiled. "You know me." He lifted her, looked around.

"Now we've got a problem that we need to settle real fast. What do we do with these two bodies? We could deliver them to the sheriff at Mariposa and tell our story, but I had a bit of a run-in with the sheriff at Mariposa on my visit there—I'll tell you about that—and he might not be so understanding to see me in trouble again so soon."

"I think we bury them. Nobody know."

He nodded. They opened the dead men's sacks, pulled out a small ax and pan. He found a damp spot near the fire circle and loosened the ground with the ax, then used the pan to scoop out the soil. An hour of this labor, and he had a long shallow hole.

Using the pan and their hands, they covered the bodies and camp gear. They walked about the site, collecting rocks and downed limbs, placing them randomly on the mound of soil. Then they gathered dry leaves and sticks that they scattered on the grave and campsite, erasing any evidence of their presence.

They walked to Tahnee's horse. "Good thing you have stout reins. I wish the other horses had the same. I hope some stranger claims those horses before they find their way home, wherever that is."

He untied the reins of Tahnee's horse and handed them to her. "Let's get my horse and get back to the u-ma-cha. We've got lots to talk about."

They rode in silence in the gloaming, finding the trail with only a few false steps in surprisingly bright moonlight. Reaching the u-ma-cha in darkness, they dismounted at the animal pen.

"I'll take care of the horses." Jason said. "If you'll build a fire and get some coffee started, I want to know how you got into that mess, and I'll tell you what I've been doing. If you're interested."

She cuffed him on his arm as he danced away. "I interest. You silly. You take care horses."

By the time he got the horses fed, watered and hobbled and entered the u-ma-cha, she had built a fire, set a pan of water to heat, and laid out bread, jerky and dried plums.

He cocked his head. "Where did you get this?" he said.

"I take from bags before we bury bags with bodies."

He patted her on the head. "Smart lady." He sat beside her, and they ate. He told her all that had happened to him since that day when Savage's men had forced him to return to Mariposa with them.

Then it was her turn. She told about being surprised outside the u-ma-cha by the two men. They asked her what she was doing here, whether others were with her. She pretended not to understand English, and they did not persist. They simply let her know that she was going with them. When she resisted, one of the men slapped her hard and pointed toward her saddle that he had dragged from the u-ma-cha. The other man went inside the u-ma-cha and came out, carrying the rifle. She said that during the ride, she rode slowly until the rider following her struck her back with his quirt, then struck the horse on the rump.

"I not afraid, Jay-son. I know you come for me."

He smiled, kissed her.

Sitting at the fire, staring into the flames, they talked softly, glancing occasionally through the u-ma-cha opening to the black void outside and up at the circular wall of the interior that was dimly illuminated by the fire.

He went outside and walked away from the clearing to relieve himself, then returned to the u-ma-cha to find her sitting on the blankets, naked but for an unbuttoned shirt she wore. He undressed and they slid under the covers, searching, fumbling and writhing in their passion. Finally, spent, he lay on his back, breathing heavily, looking into the darkness at the top of the u-ma-cha where wisps of smoke from the fire seeped through the crevices at the peak.

He turned on his side to face her. "Tell me a Yosemite story," he said.

She lay on her side, facing him. Leaning over, she kissed him, rolled over on her back. "A story." She closed her eyes a long moment, opened them, looked up to the dark peak.

"Okay. Kos-su-kah, young chief of Ahwahneechee love a beautiful young woman name Tis-sa-ack. They want to marry, and parents agree. Everyone happy. Tis-sa-ack and friends gather acorns, seeds, wild fruits and roots to make feast. Kos-su-kah and friends go on big hunt up in mountains get meat for feast. He supposed to go to edge of cliff at sunset and shoot arrow to valley to show hunt finished. Tis-sa-ack say she go to valley to watch for arrow. When hunt finished, Kos-su-kah go to cliff top to shoot arrow. Before he can shoot arrow, cliff edge break off, and he fall to his death on rocks at bottom.

"Tis-sa-ack wait and wait for arrow, all evening, all night, but it not come. No arrow. Next morning, Tis-sa-ack climb mountain to place where he supposed to shoot arrow. She look over side and see his body on rocks at bottom of cliff. She surprise, she hurt so much. She build big fire, signal people come help. They come, lower her on rope to body. They raise body and Tis-sa-ack up to cliff top. She fall on body, cry and cry, lie on body. She stop crying. People try raise her, but she dead.

"Tis-sa-ack die of broken heart. Her spirit and her lover spirit, they go El-o-win, spirit land other side of sun going down. People take bodies to valley, burn bodies, scatter ashes in winds of Ah-wah-nee, valley they love so much."

She rolled over to face him. He breathed evenly, eyes closed. She kissed his cheek, pulled the blanket up.

They stood outside the u-ma-cha the next morning at first light. They looked up at the lacy snowflakes swirling in the bare treetops. The cloud cover was low, gunmetal gray.

"I wanted to move today," he said, "but that might not be a good idea."

"It look like more snow come. I think we better stay u-ma-cha another day."

They stooped and entered, sat at the fire circle. He added sticks to the fire while she poured coffee into two cups. They sat silent, studying the flames.

Still staring into the fire, she spoke softly. "Jason, who 'Jessie?'"

He turned abruptly to her. "How . . ."

"You talk in sleep. You say 'Jessie . . . Jessie.' You roll head, sound like you going to cry. I touch you, and then you quiet."

He leaned back, looked up. "Ah, Tahnee." He looked back to the fire. And told her everything. Jessie, Christian, Nicole. The Kentucky farm and the decision to go to Oregon. The fire at Independence, killing the arsonist. His desperate attempt to escape, anywhere, joining Paul and Andy for California, the jumping off place of the world, he once called it.

"You know the rest," he said. He wiped his eyes with a sleeve.

She took his arm and leaned on a shoulder. "I sorry, Jay-son."

He stared into the fire, put his arm around her and pulled her close. "You saved my life, Tahnee. If I had not found you, I would have found some way to end my life."

She squeezed his arm, and they sat quiet, at peace, listening to the wind in the trees, watching the snowflakes through the u-ma-cha opening.

"Jay-son." She looked from the u-ma-cha opening back to the fire.

He looked at her, waiting.

"I married before. You remember story I tell you, 'bout young man and woman, he fall off cliff and die?" He nodded. "Something like that happen me. I marry very young, 'bout fifteen. Indian girl marry very young, some fourteen, fifteen. He and friends go mountain for hunt. They shoot deer, and deer fall over side of cliff, catch on rock. He climb down with rope to deer so they can pull deer up. He tie rope to deer, but he fall away, die on rocks at bottom of cliff. I so sad, I want die, want to jump over cliff, but friends pull me away from edge.

"I never happy again . . . till I meet you." She held his arm tightly. "Jay-son, you save my life too."

# Chapter13

After three days of sub-freezing temperatures and a light snowfall, the weather broke. They awoke to a clear sky and weak sunshine. Though a crisp cold breeze still blew, they agreed that it was time to move.

"If we can feel a change in the season," Jason said, "Savage will feel it even more in Mariposa. The battalion might already be moving. We want to stay ahead of them."

While Tahnee packed bags, Jason saddled the horses, then led them and the mule to the u-ma-cha entrance. Tahnee helped him tie the loaded bags on the mule.

By mid-morning, they stood silent, holding reins, looking at the u-ma-cha, now empty, the embers of their last fire already cold in the fire circle.

"I love this u-ma-cha," Tahnee said. "I very happy here."

Jason encircled her shoulders with an arm. "We'll have another one you will love just as much."

She took his face in her hands and kissed him. "Okay, you say so."

They mounted and rode down the slope, Jason holding the lead on the mule. The snow pack on the slope was no more than a foot deep, but on reaching the main trail in the swale, it was deeper, and the animals had a harder time. Jason turned back upslope, Tahnee following, and they rode at the edge of timber. Though the path they followed now was not as level as that in the swale, it was easier going because of less snow.

They rode in silence, listening to forest sounds, occasional birdcalls, the whispering breeze in the tops of pines, the mournful howl of a wolf. Dropping into a ravine, they surprised two does that bounded away, crashing through a manzanita thicket in their flight. Often, the riders stopped to let their animals rest, then proceeded, up and down on the forest trail, moving higher on the mountain.

"Hey, up there!" They stopped, looked back and below. Three men sat their horses in the main trail. "Hold up! We need to talk to you!"

"Who they?" Tahnee said to Jason.

"Dunno. We can't run in this stuff, so we wait."

The three riders turned their mounts and moved up from the swale to the higher path. They pulled up beside Jason and Tahnee.

"I'll be damned. It is you." The speaker was Kelly. "You're easier to find than I expected."

"Kelly," said Jason. "You again. This isn't by chance, is it?"

"Nope. Sheriff Burney wants to talk to you."

"Burney? What about?"

"Dunno. He said he needed to talk to you. Didn't say why? Official business though. He made me a deputy to come get you."

"A deputy? Are you arresting me?"

"He said he needed to talk with you. That's all I know. We need to go now."

Jason looked at Tahnee, hesitated. He turned to Kelly. "Lead off, deputy."

*****

"Well, here we are again. Didn't expect to see you again so soon," Sheriff Burney said.

"I might say the same," said Jason.

Jason and Tahnee sat in the sheriff's office with Burney and Kelly. "Now I suppose you want to know why I had you brought in," Burney said.

"That question did cross my mind."

"Last time we talked, you said you owned a Leman that had a sloppy carving of a buck head on the stock." Burney leaned back, pushed a couple of hanging coats aside, and grasped a rifle. He laid Jason's Leman on the desk. "Look something like this?"

Jason's eyes opened wide as he leaned over the desk. "By damn! That's my Leman! Where did you find it?"

"Where did you lose it?"

"It was stolen from our camp when we were out checking the trail."

"When was this?"

Jason looked at Tahnee. "When was it?" he said. "Six days? Seven days?"

Tahnee played the game. She closed her eyes, opened them. "Hmm. I think five days."

"Where did you find it?" said Jason.

"We didn't find it. It found us. This horse came walking right into the middle of Mariposa two days ago. Stopped at the Hideout hitching post and just stood there, reins hanging. We figured that horse had spent a good deal of time at that very spot, so we talked with the bartender and patrons of the Hideout. The word is that the owner of the animal is a regular customer named Ed Farmer, and Ed ain't been seen for some days."

The sheriff leaned back in his chair, waiting. When Jason did not respond, he leaned forward, put his elbows on the desk and looked hard at Jason. "Since that horse had no rider, I took him with me. And what did I spy on that horse but a Leman, almost new. Like the one you said you owned. With the sloppy carving on the stock."

Burney and Jason stared at each other, waiting.

"Sheriff, somebody stole that rifle from our camp. I haven't seen it since, not till you produced it just now. Where is this, Ed Farmer, you said?"

"Thought you might tell me." The sheriff leaned back, waited. When Jason did not respond, he continued. "This is the second time you've been in my office on the possibility of being mixed up in some serious business. Is that just by chance? I don't want to arrest you. I don't have any hard evidence, and I don't want to hold you. But I gotta look into this matter, and you need to stick around in case I want to talk to you."

Jason grimaced, looked at Tahnee, glanced at the window, then back to Burney. "Sheriff, I'm going to tell you something I haven't told anybody except Bess and Billy. Tahnee is a Yosemite. She was captured and held as a slave in Sacramento and the diggings for almost two years. I found her and told her I would help her return to her village. We want to warn her people before the battalion gets there. We're not going to encourage them to resist. We just want them to have time to think about what they are going to do when the battalion arrives.

"I'm not running away from you. If you'll let me be on my way, we'll be in the path and eventually in the camps of the battalion. If you need to talk with me again, send word with the same riders who will carry your messages to the battalion."

Burney frowned, looked through the front windows to the empty road in front of the office. Jason stole a glance at Tahnee who pursed her lips.

Burney looked back at Jason. "Okay. I believe you. Sounds like a good plan, actually. There's a bunch of hell-raisin' Indian-haters in the battalion, and it might be wise for the Yosemites to know what to expect." Burney stood, picked up the rifle, offered it to Jason.

Jason took the rifle, extended his hand, and they shook. "Thanks, Sheriff. Let's hope all this has a happy outcome, though I fear for the Yosemites, and all the other mountain Indians."

"Well said. I have to admit that I'll need to side with the townspeople if it ever comes to a showdown, but I have to agree that the Indians are gettin' the short end of the stick in all this. Don't tell anybody I said so."

Burney went to the door and opened it. Jason went out, followed by Tahnee and Kelly.

Burney stepped outside. "You say you 'found' this purty Indian woman?" He glanced at Tahnee, smiled.

Jason glanced at Tahnee. "Well, I found her at a placer upstream from mine where her owner was abusing her. I beat hell out of him and took her."

"That's more like it," said Burney, smiling. He sobered. "My contacts with the battalion will let you know if I need to talk with you. Now you better be off. Savage has the members of the battalion in one place, I hear, and they'll be moving out any day now."

*****

Jason and Tahnee left Mariposa in late afternoon, riding on a trail that had been beaten down by unknown riders after the last light snowfall. On leaving the sheriff's office, they had talked about spending the night with Bess and Billy, but the sheriff's report that the battalion was leaving soon convinced them they should leave immediately.

They camped that night at an open spot in a heavy stand of sugar pine in the low foothills. Breaking camp next morning at first light, they continued the ride up the swale. Jason rode at the head, and Tahnee followed, holding the lead of the mule.

The gray overcast at sunup lifted, dissipated, and was replaced by a silver blue sky without a cloud in sight. They moved through a succession of heavy forests and sunny glades, on rocky passages that looked down into deep canyons, wooded on one side and the other a rocky slope devoid of vegetation of any sort.

When the sun was high overhead, Jason pulled up, looked down the back trail, squinted, listening. A faint, distant sound from below, like soft rolling thunder.

"I hear it," said Tahnee, "not weather."

"No, not weather. That's rifle shots. Lots of shots."

They sat their horses, motionless, quiet, listening. The shots faded to an occasional pop, then it was quiet but for the soft sounds of a light breeze in the nearby pines. They turned forward and moved on, up the mountainside.

They rode through a thick, cold pine forest, pushing low limbs aside, and across openings where bright sunshine had melted most of the snow.

They were passing through a heavy stand of ponderosa pine when suddenly the bark on a tree trunk beside Jason shattered, followed instantly by the distant sound of a rifle shot. Then the sound of another shot. He searched down the slope for the source of the fire.

"Stay back!" he said softly over his shoulder to Tahnee. "Go back in the trees!"

Jason heard a faint, but clear shout down the slope. "Did you get him?"

Then a faint response. "Don't know. Do you see him?"

Jason rode at a walk from the cover of the pines, a hand in the air. He shouted in the direction of the shots. "Hey! Why are you shooting? Who are you?"

A man rose slowly from behind a downed tree trunk, holding a rifle pointed at Jason. "Who the hell are you?" the figure said. "What're you doing here?"

"I'm a miner. I'm hunting. Who the hell are you?"

Another man rose from behind cover, holding a rifle. Then another, and another.

"Hell, we thought you was an Indian. Come on down." Jason glanced aside, confirmed that Tahnee was not in sight. He turned his horse down the slope, pulled up in front of the four men.

"I was just about to bag a doe that is probably halfway to Stockton by now," said Jason.

"Sorry 'bout that," the shooter said. "We been chasing hostiles and thought you was the one we was chasing."

"Hostiles? How do you know they're hostiles?"

"We had a run-in with a bunch down the hill, and they run off. Mr. Savage sent us to chase some that run off this way. You didn't see any skedaddling Indians?"

"No, didn't see any. You're with the battalion?" said Jason.

"Yeah, you know about the battalion then."

"I was down in Mariposa a while back. Are you having any luck?"

"Hell yeah. We talked a couple of villages into goin' down to the reservation on their own. Another bunch needed some persuading. We killed a dozen and burned everything they owned, and they decided, what th' hell, they would go to the reservation." The other men laughed.

"C'mon, Scottie, we gotta get back," said one of the others. "Mr. Savage'll figure we got lost or got wiped out."

"Take care of yourself," the shooter said to Jason. "Hostiles ain't exactly like deer. They shoot back." He snickered and joined the others who were already making their way on foot down the heavily forested slope.

Jason waited until the four had disappeared. Then he walked his horse up the slope to the edge of the thicket. Tahnee rode out beside him. He told her about the encounter with the hostile hunters.

"We can move faster than the full battalion," he said, "but there will be advance parties that we may yet run into. We need to move faster."

The next day was a continuation of the last. They woke at first light and were back on the trail in minutes under a clear sky and a cold light northerly.

On a particularly steep rocky hillside, almost devoid of snow, they dismounted and led their horses.

In minutes, Jason was puffing. He stopped, sat down on a rock. He removed his hat, wiped his face with a sleeve.

"Whoo. What's wrong with me. I'm exhausted."

"It very high here in mountain. I think you live before in low country. Indian people from low country have trouble when they come to high mountain."

"Didn't know that." He stood, looked up. "I think we can ride now." They mounted and rode up the trail into a shady stand of lodgepole pine on a flat.

"Stop!" Tahnee said softly. Jason reined in and looked at Tahnee. She pointed across a low swale below.

Jason saw them. A party of a dozen riders moved through a thicket of trees and low bushes. They were but shadows that appeared in the open spaces in the forest as they moved ahead, disappeared behind the huge trees, then reappeared.

"Indian," Tahnee whispered, still watching the moving shadows.

The riders left the trees and moved in the open down the opposite slope toward the trail in the swale below.

Tahnee's eyes opened wide. "Jason! My people!" She reined to the right and rode slowly down the slope, her horse occasionally sliding in the slush.

"*Tahnee,*" Jason called softly. "Are you sure?"

"Yes," she called over her shoulder. "I think."

"You *think,*" Jason mumbled to himself. He reined downslope after her, pulling the mule along.

The six riders stopped when they saw Tahnee and Jason approaching. Two riders pulled rifles slowly from scabbards, held them loosely, watching.

Tahnee called in Miwok: "I am Tah-nee-hay, Ahwahneechee!" The riders lowered the rifles. One raised a hand in greeting. The six waited, watched Jason and Tahnee ride to them.

"I know you," the leader said in Miwok. "Your father thinks you are dead."

While Jason looked on in bewilderment and admiration, Tahnee spoke rapidly, gesturing frequently toward him. He assumed that she was telling the riders the story of her two years since leaving her home that fateful day. She told about Jason, a good white man who rescued her and now was committed with her to warn her people of the plan to force them to move from Ah-wah-nee to the reservation in the valley. At least that's what he assumed she was saying.

The leader had listened without interrupting. Then he spoke. "I understand. I am glad to know you are safe, and the people will be happy to see you. Now I must tell you, Tah-nee-hay. The whites are coming. We were hunting in the foothills when we were approached by armed white men who told us that all of the mountain Indians must move to a place in the valley on Fresno River that has been set aside for mountain Indians. We have never heard of this.

"When the white men learned that we are Yosemites, the leader told us to go to our home and tell the chief to come meet them and talk. The white leader said that his party was part of a large force that is riding toward the home of the Yosemites. If the chief does not agree to talk, he said, the force will attack our villages. We said that we would tell our chief."

Tahnee explained all this to Jason. He pondered. The battalion had moved faster than he thought possible in the snow.

"We go now," said the leader. He and his companions moved off, and Tahnee and Jason followed.

*****

Tahnee and Jason rode behind the leader of the party. The others were strung out behind them. They climbed higher and higher, sometimes dropping into a swale and up the other side, always upward. They had ridden until near darkness the previous night and slept around a campfire. They were on the trail this morning at first light.

Jason glanced at Tahnee, riding at his side. They had hardly spoken this morning. But now he sensed her growing excitement with each hour, each mile. She looked side to side, back to Jason. She rode straight in her saddle, bending right, left. She looked at him, wide-eyed, tense.

"I know this place. I remember," she said, over and over. "I know this place."

At high noon, they reached what appeared to be a summit and began a steady, gradual decline. They rode on a dim game trail in a heavy pine forest, the trail carpeted with a thick layer of needles.

Her excitement grew. She appeared nervous, apprehensive. "I know this place, I know this place."

Suddenly they emerged from the forest onto an open flat.

Jason was stunned. Far below, a broad valley stretched miles to the distant end. The floor was covered with a carpet of dense forests, broken by grassy meadows, a river snaking down the center. On each side of the valley, high stone walls rose almost vertically from the floor. Lacy waterfalls flowed over the edges of cliffs on both sides of the valley, promising deluges with the beginning of snow melt. The valley narrowed at the far end where a high stony pinnacle appeared to be sheared off, as if cut by a cosmic knife.

Jason dismounted and walked to a point that gave an unobstructed view of the valley. Tahnee dismounted and came up to stand beside him. She put an arm around his waist.

Jason turned to her. "This is your home?"

She smiled. "This Ah-wah-nee. My home."

Jason looked back at the valley, the soaring cliffs and thin streams spilling over the edges, the flow scattered by air currents flowing upward at the sheer cliffs. He was dumbstruck.

*If there is a heaven, it must look something like this.*

The six Indians, still mounted, set off down a trail that led from the flat toward the valley floor below. Jason and Tahnee mounted hurriedly and followed.

Reaching the valley floor an hour later, they rode on a trail beside the river, through lush groves of yellow pines and sugar pines, silver firs and spruce, magnificent sequoias, seeming to pierce the sky. The trail meandered through the woods and open places, in half sunshine and half shade. The snow cover was heavier in the deep shade, less in the sunny places. Thin rivulets of melt water flowed in trickles from the shady spots.

Leaving the forests, they rode in a broad, open grassy meadow that was marked by only a few scattered oaks. At the far end, below the peak that had been sheared off, they entered a village of dozens of u-ma-cha that were arrayed around an open area. A large gathering of people stood in the open space, watching the riders come. The people stared at Jason, frowning, whispering to each other.

When the riders had almost reached the people, Tahnee's eyes opened wide, and her hand went to her mouth. "Jay-son. My father."

They drew up before the people, and Tahnee slid off her horse. She ran to the man who stood at the front. They clasped hands as she talked rapidly. Villagers crowded around and listened, glancing often at Jason.

Jason dismounted and waited. As she talked with her father, Tahnee often looked back at Jason. Finally she came to him and told him about their conversation. She had told her father and the others what had happened to her since that fateful day when her friend and she had left the valley. She told them about Jason and all that he had done for her.

Tahnee tugged his arm, and they walked to her father.

"Jason, this Chief Tenaya. He is my father. He say thank you for helping me. He say he want talk with you, but first he must talk with riders we meet on trail."

Tenaya nodded to Jason, raised a hand in a greeting, and walked to the leader of the riders they had met and ridden with. Chief Tenaya motioned for Tahnee to come, and she walked with him. As they talked, she glanced over her shoulder at Jason.

The parley broke up, men walking away in twos and singly. Tahnee came to Jason.

"It is very bad. White men say many men come to make Indians move to place called reservation in valley near Mariposa. They say everything they need is there. Food, clothes, place to live. They tell men to tell Chief Tenaya to come talk with white leader name Savage. They tell leader of band where to meet on trail above valley."

"What is the chief going to do?"

"He say he will go and talk with Savage. He want me to go with him. You too. He say maybe you and I help, explain why we want stay here in Ah-wah-nee. Will you go with us? Will it be trouble for you?"

"I will go, but I'm not sure it will help. Savage knows me. He saw me in San Jose, and he knows how I feel about all this. He probably knows about the trouble I had in Mariposa. If you still want me to go, I will."

"Yes, I want you go."

# Chapter 14

Chief Tenaya walked down a rocky trail at the head of a dozen men. Tahnee and Jason walked at the back. They looked down on an encampment in a clearing bordered by towering Ponderosa pines, morning campfires still smoldering.

Beside a fire circle, a half dozen men stood behind Major Savage. The men were armed with rifles, some held loosely in the crook of an arm, others resting the butts on the ground. All watched the approach of the Yosemites and, curiously, a white man.

Chief Tenaya and the others stopped in front of Savage. Tahnee walked up beside Tenaya. Jason stood behind the other Yosemites, unsure whether he should contribute or try to be invisible.

Greetings and introductions were exchanged. Tahnee began to translate, but Savage smiled and replied in the Miwok language, imperfectly but understandable.

Savage explained that the whites wanted peace with the Yosemites. He said that Tenaya must go to Mariposa to see the commissioners and enter into a treaty with them. Then the Yosemites would move to the Fresno reservation where the Great Father would provide everything for his people. Food, homes, clothing, all they need. There would be peace forever and no more war. Savage smiled, a practiced, forced smile.

Tenaya replied that his people were content in their valley. Why should they wish to leave? They wanted nothing from the white Great Father. The Yosemites' Great Spirit provided all their needs, and they wanted nothing from the whites.

"Go now," Tenaya said. "We will stay in the mountains where we were born, where our fathers' ashes were sown to the winds, where we have all we shall ever need. I have finished." He turned to leave.

"Chief Tenaya," said Savage. Tenaya stopped and turned back. "If you have all you need in your valley, why do your people steal animals and goods from the miners and burn their homes? Why do you attack our posts and kill our people? It was your people who attacked my own stores and stole my goods and killed my people. I have been a friend of all the tribes for many years, and this is the way the tribes respond to my friendship."

Chief Tenaya pondered. "What you say has merit. In our culture, when someone wrongs us, we respond. The whites chase away the game; they cut down our acorn trees; they kill our people. In our culture, it is okay to do to enemies these things that you say my people do. If you say that the whites are not our enemies, then we will not do these things, and we will live in peace with them."

Tenaya's face hardened. "But we will not go to the reservation. I have heard about the tribes who have gone there. They are bad people. They have attacked us. They are our enemies. We could not live in peace with them at the reservation. Here in Ah-wah-nee, we can defend ourselves."

Savage was furious. "No! That will not do! You must go to the commissioners and make a treaty. If you do not do this, your men will continue to attack the whites, steal from us and kill our people. If you do not go to the commissioners, we will destroy your tribe. Your villages will be burned, and your people will die, and your tribe will be but a memory. I promise you that!"

Tenaya did not flinch. He stood silent, head lowered, as if studying the ground at his feet. He looked up. "All right. I am told that the whites are as plentiful as the raindrops and stronger than the north wind. I will do as you say. I will go to my people and talk with them. We will do what we must do for the move to this place that you have set aside for us. I will bring my people here in three days." He walked away, head held high, and the others, including Jason and Tahnee, followed.

"Bishop, isn't it?" said Savage. Jason and Tahnee stopped, turned around to face Savage. "I remember you from San Jose, and I've heard about your problems in Mariposa. What are you doing here?"

"Curiosity, I suppose. I wondered why people whose ancestors lived in this valley since the beginning of time all of a sudden have to leave. Why is that, Major?"

Savage clenched his eyes, opened them and squinted at this interloper. "Bishop, you're a stranger, and you have no idea what's going on here. A lot has changed since the beginning of time. Many people in authority, including the Governor of California, want to solve the Indian problem by exterminating them, literally killing every last one of them. I don't hold to that. I have dealt peacefully with Indians for years, but things have changed. We have to accept the present condition. The only acceptable way to have peace is to make agreements that will remove the friction between tribes and whites."

"And you'll do that by turning the Indians into a class of paupers to be cared for by the whites?"

Savage looked down, shook his head, looked up. "That's really a stupid statement. I don't know what your interest is in these people, though I can guess." He glanced at Tahnee. "If you care about these people, Bishop, you'll go to their village and persuade them to make a treaty with the commissioners. If you think that's a bad idea, maybe I should just arrest you right now for being part of a bunch of hostiles."

Jason squared his shoulders and glared at Savage. Tahnee tugged his sleeve, and he turned and walked with her toward Tenaya and the others who were ahead on the trail to Ah-wah-nee.

Jason and Tahnee strolled in the village beneath the mountain with the split dome. She showed him the meetinghouse, which had the appearance of a large u-ma-cha, and the sweat lodge, a structure of planks and logs, covered with earth.

"What are all these raised bins beside u-ma-cha?" said Jason.

Tahnee described the cha'ka, a granary for storing the acorns that were gathered in autumn. The cha'ka had the appearance of a basket, several feet tall, constructed of upright poles with branches woven to form sides and thatched with a roof of fir or cedar to protect the nuts from rain. The inside was lined with pine needles and wormwood to discourage deer and rodents from sampling the acorns. Each family had its own cha'ka.

They continued walking. Tahnee spoke occasionally to women at their u-ma-cha. While Tahnee wore a dress of soft decorated deerskin, most of the women wore an unadorned buckskin skirt that reached halfway between the knee and the ankle, with a fringe of several inches at the bottom. A buckskin wrap was worn over the upper body. The few men they encountered wore a simple buckskin breech-clout, which hung as an apron in front and back. Most men and women wore no footwear, though some, like Tahnee, wore moccasins. A few wore blankets of dressed animal skins wrapped around shoulders. Most children as old as ten wore nothing.

Passing a family group that sat at a fire pit, pulling bits of flesh from a fish that had been roasted on the coals, Jason turned to Tahnee. "It's the middle of the afternoon. What meal are they eating?"

"Yosemite people eat when hungry, not three times every day like white people. They might eat a little bit five times a day, or only one time. Just when hungry. Better than white way." She smiled. They passed another u-ma-cha where a woman watched a rabbit that lay on the glowing embers. The carcass had been skinned, cut open, entrails removed and replaced by hot coals.

"Hmm. Interesting," said Jason.

They stopped at an u-ma-cha. "My father say this our u-ma-cha," Tahnee said. "He say tell him what we need, and he will send." They stooped and went inside. A large basket of acorns and smaller baskets of foods and supplies were arrayed around the perimeter. In the center, a shallow pit and stone fire circle.

"Jay-son, my father talk with tribe leaders now, decide what to do. I not sure he plan to go with Savage. I think he will go to Savage tomorrow or day after, tell him we need more time. If he goes to talk, I go with him."

"I think I should not go. Savage knows how I feel about all this, and I just make him angry."

"Okay, you stay here u-ma-cha. I go." She brightened. "I have idea. You say you want taste acorn bread. Maybe you make acorn bread while I am away."

"What? I don't—"

"Oh. You don't know how make acorn bread?" She smiled. "Okay, I show you. Here, bring acorns." She pointed to a basket filled with acorns among the food baskets. She picked up a large empty basket and a stack of three empty smaller baskets.

Carrying the acorn basket, Jason followed Tahnee through the village. About three dozen u-ma-cha were scattered about, and Tahnee said there were more u-ma-cha at other sites nearby. She spoke to women who were busy with everyday chores, dressing or painting a deerskin, carrying an armful of firewood, cooking, watching children at play. No one appeared to be preparing for a move from the valley.

He looked up at the sky. Deep blue, clear but for wispy clouds at the eastern horizon. The only sounds were distant bird song, the muffled conversation of three women seated before an u-ma-cha, the soft laughter of children playing a stick game beside another u-ma-cha. Streams on the heights on each side of the valley flowed over the edges of cliffs and plunged noiselessly to disappear in forests at the base of the walls.

He remembered Tenaya's comment to Savage. We have all we need in our valley, he said. Why should we wish to leave? *Why indeed?*

At the edge of the village, they stopped at a grinding site in a grove of oaks. The granite slab was marked with a score of shallow holes where Yosemite women for generations had ground acorns with stone pestles. A narrow, shallow stream flowed in the oak grove nearby.

They sat down beside a hole. "Okay, now I teach you cook acorns." Following her instruction, they cracked and shelled the acorns, discarded the bad nuts and dumped the acorns into a grinding hole. With a stone pestle, she pounded and ground the nuts to a fine yellow meal. Using a soaproot brush, she retrieved acorn fragments that flew in all directions with each stroke of the pestle.

While Tahnee was busy with the pounding, Jason gathered firewood and built a fire. He frowned when she told him to gather some small stones and drop them into the fire.

"Why?" he said.

She cocked her head. "You know how cook acorns?"

"Uh . . . no." He picked up a basket, went to the stream and collected a number of stones. He walked back to the fire and emptied the basket into the flames.

"Here," she said, offering him an empty basket. "Get water from stream."

"Get water? In a basket?"

"Yes. That what I said."

"Ooh, yes, ma'am." He smiled, looked at the basket, cocked his head. The basket was woven with grass fibers as hard and strong as wire. It appeared to be treated with some sort of waxy compound. Tahnee later explained that Yosemites coated their baskets with soaproot juice, which hardened to a glue-like consistency.

Jason walked to the stream, dipped the basket into the water and lifted it. Drops fell from the basket bottom, then almost stopped. "Hmm, never saw a basket-bucket." He stood by the stream, studying the basket.

"Come now," Tahnee called. "Keep fire hot over stones. Put basket on ground beside fire."

He walked to the fire, set the water basket down. "I don't understand what's happening." He picked up sticks from the pile and tossed them on the fire.

"I show you. Wait."

After a few minutes more, she scooped the meal from the grinding hole and dumped it into a hard-packed sand basin adjacent to the grinding slab. With two sticks, she lifted the hot stones from the fire and dropped them into the basket of water. The water bubbled, and steam rose.

"We wait until water is hot," she said.

After a few minutes, following her instruction, Jason removed the stones from the basket and then poured hot water repeatedly over the meal to seep into and through the sand beneath.

"This take away bitter taste," she said, flexing her back, stretching. "I not do this for long time. My back hurt."

When the leaching was finished, she stirred the pulverized meal and separated it into three baskets, according to size of the meal. She explained that she would make soup with the finest meal. The meal with the middle consistency would be used to make mush. With the grainiest meal, she would make patties.

"Patties are like bread," she said. "This my favorite acorn food."

That evening, they finished their meal with acorn patties cooked on flat rocks heated in the fire. "Umm, so good," she said. "First I have in long, long time. Do you like?"

"I do. Different, but good."

*****

At first light the next day, Tahnee went with Chief Tenaya and a few others to the battalion's camp on the slopes above the valley. They returned at dusk. Tahnee told Jason about the meeting.

Savage had watched the Yosemites approach. He said nothing when Tenaya walked to him. He waited. The Chief told Savage that he had consulted with tribal leaders, and they agreed that they would meet with the commissioners who were representatives of the white Great Father who was so good and powerful and rich. Tenaya said that he would bring his people to him the next day, and they would move to the reservation. Savage was pleased, called Tenaya a wise leader and said that he would bring peace and a good life to his people.

A fierce storm blew in that night, dumping a foot of snow on the valley floor and more on the slopes. With a few others, Tenaya went to the battalion's camp the next morning where he explained that the people could not move with their goods in such weather. Savage was not satisfied, but he acknowledged the difficulty in moving in the snow. The storm is already moderating, he said to Tenaya, and you must bring your people tomorrow. Tenaya agreed.

Next morning, Tenaya with a few others, including Tahnee, went to the battalion's camp. Savage grew increasingly agitated as he watched Tenaya approach. Savage asked him where were his people. Tenaya explained that the snows were still too deep for them to move their goods since they would be leaving Ah-wah-nee forever and must carry everything they own.

Savage's patience was at an end. He said that he knew the Chief was stalling and that he was ready to take the battalion to the valley to uproot the Yosemites and force their removal. Tenaya tried to convince Savage that his horses would founder in the snow, and if they were able to reach the valley, the rocks were so large and the stony hills so treacherous that they would not be able to climb out of the valley.

Savage brushed Tenaya's pleas aside and told him that he had just one more chance to settle this peacefully. If the Chief did not bring his people tomorrow, Savage said he would order the battalion to march to the valley and remove the people by force. All villages would be completely destroyed, and any people who resisted would be killed.

Jason sat on the ground before their u-ma-cha, watching Tahnee and the others walking into the village. She sat down beside Jason. "They are coming to Ah-wah-nee. What are we going to do?"

"We must wait to see what Chief Tenaya plans. He must have known that the battalion eventually would come to the valley for your people."

The rest of the day, Tenaya and the other leaders walked about the village, talking with the people. Then they assembled in the meetinghouse to decide how to respond to Savage's demands.

At noon the next day, a crowd of Ahwahneechee, led by Chief Tenaya, walked from the valley to the battalion's encampment. When Savage saw them coming, he came out and counted them as they passed his tent. The group stopped and huddled outside the camp, awaiting instructions.

Savage walked to Tenaya and Tahnee. Jason stood in the midst of the group of Ahwahneechee, trying to avoid notice.

"Where are the others?" said Savage. "I count but seventy-two. I know you have hundreds more."

Tenaya swept his hand to encompass the huddled group. "These are all my people who are willing to go with me to the plains. Many of the people in my village are from other tribes, Paiute, Mono, Yokut, Maidu. They married Yosemite women and now they have taken their wives and children and returned to their own tribes."

"You do not tell the truth, Chief Tenaya. They could not go over the mountains during the snows. They are still in your valley or hiding in the mountains. I know this.

"Go with your people now to the reservation. I have assigned men to lead you. I will take my force to your valley. If we find more of your people in the valley or in the mountains who are willing to join you, we will bring them to the reservation. If they refuse to come, you will not see them again. They will be killed." He turned to his officers and ordered the march to begin.

The Yosemites moved off on the westward trail toward the valley and their new home, following their escort. Tahnee stood with Tenaya. "Father, what am I to do?"

"What your heart tells you. I don't think the white chief will make you come with us. I believe he does not think of you as one of us."

Tears streamed down her cheeks. "Father, I am Ahwahneechee."

"Daughter, we must go now, but maybe this is not forever. The white man thinks only of today. He does not understand the meaning of time, and he has no attachment to the earth. We will always hope to return to our home, to Ah-wah-nee. Until then, go with Jason. He is a good man."

She watched her father, Chief Tenaya, as he joined the people on the journey that would take them to a new life on the reservation in the valley set aside for them by the white Great Father. She walked to Jason, her face clouded. She had no more tears. He took her in his arms and held her.

They parted and slipped into the forest where they would find the trail back to Ah-wah-nee.

Major Savage followed a young man whom Tenaya had assigned to lead the battalion to the villages of the Yosemites. The mounted volunteers were strung out behind, making slow progress through the thin snow pack down the slope toward the valley.

When the column emerged from the pine forest on the point overlooking the valley, the riders were dumbstruck. They sat their horses in awe, jaws hanging. Some dismounted and walked to the overlook, leaving their horses with reins trailing. The volunteers stood there, silenced by the spectacular view.

Major Savage stood with Captain Boling, second in command of the battalion, staring at the valley. Both held the reins of their horses. "Old Tenaya is a fox," said Savage. "He described his home as a miserable place. Made it sound like someplace you sure wouldn't want to see."

Boling nodded. After a long moment, "I understand his reluctance to leave. I almost sympathize with him."

Savage looked aside at Boling. "You might not feel so if some savage decides he wants your hair. I have no confidence in Tenaya's saying that there are none of his people around."

They mounted, and Savage ordered the march to continue. Volunteers found their horses and mounted, falling into a column that wound its way through low brush and scrub pine down the slope.

Reaching the valley floor, the battalion rode through a thick pine forest that opened occasionally to a grassy meadow. The warming sun cast long shadows through the pine boughs. Riders marveled at a thin waterfall on the south wall, the breeze whipping the light flow into a watery lace.

At sunset, the volunteers camped in a grove of large oaks on the banks of a river, swollen from snowmelt and overflowing low banks on both sides. A search for a ford had proven fruitless. The Yosemite guide told Savage that the melt in the high country would decrease during the cold night, and they would find a crossing the following morning.

Around the campfire that evening, there was a spirited discussion of what to name the valley, as if the valley had no name. Paradise Valley was suggested and debated. Others offered scriptural names, romantic names and foreign names. Doctor Lafayette Bunnell, medical officer of the battalion, argued that the choice should be an American name, both descriptive and evocative. He proposed the valley be named Yosemite, thereby perpetuating the identity of the Indians who were being forced to leave the valley, their ancestral home, never to return.

The suggestion was met with catcalls, laughter and angry shouts. "Devil take the Indians and their names!" said one. "Why do you want to perpetuate the names of murderers and thieves?" said another to a clamor of agreement.

Bunnell persisted. He spoke eloquently about a people's attachment to home and the tragedy of losing it, whatever we might think of those people. The Indians are no more a danger to anyone, he said, and we should ponder the passing of a culture. His argument silenced the dissenters, and a subdued murmur of agreement followed.

A listener who appeared to be particularly touched by Bunnell's delivery called for a vote, and by an almost unanimous count, the valley was named: Yosemite.

Jason and Tahnee sat at the back of the throng that crowded around the fire circle. They had wandered into the camp at sunset. Some volunteers smiled and spoke to Jason; others frowned or glared. Jason was tolerated by the volunteers simply because he was white, though they wondered about his association with the Indian woman. The leaders didn't know how to treat him, this miner who turned up at the strangest times, so they did nothing.

Sitting in near darkness on the outskirts of the gathering, Tahnee leaned toward Jason, spoke softly. "My people sometime call ourselves 'Yosemite' because it mean 'grizzly,' but they never called our valley 'Yosemite.' We say Ah-wah-nee. But now the whites can call our valley what they want. The Ahwahneechee now are strangers in this valley." She rested her head on Jason's shoulder, then turned her head and buried her face in the folds of his coat, sobbing.

He raised her head, kissed her, and they walked into the oak grove where their horses were tied.

# Chapter 15

At first light, the volunteers broke camp, forded the river, and rode up the valley toward the mountain whose dome was sheered off. They soon entered a village of scattered u-ma-cha, cooking fires still warm. Baskets holding stores of acorns and other foods, nuts, grass seeds, scorched grasshoppers, dried insect larvae, were inside and scattered about outside. They saw no people. The village was deserted.

Savage looked beyond the village to the mountains. "They are up there," he said to Captain Boling. "Take a force of twenty men, and see it you can find any Yosemites. If we can find a few, we will question them."

Boling organized a group of volunteers and led them to the base of the mountain. They found a number of trails where footprints led upwards on the rocky hillsides. The volunteers climbed a number of these trails but found no Indians, nor any evidence of their passage other than the footprints.

"Look out!" They looked up the hillside at the shout to see a shower of huge rocks, rolling and bouncing down the slope. Some volunteers were struck and tumbled down the hill. Others scrambled to cover behind boulders and searched the hillside for their assailants. They shot wildly at any hint of movement.

After a long silence, the volunteers slowly stood, looked up the slope and saw only stationary rocks and bushes, no Yosemites. Satisfied that the Indians had slipped away, they retreated to the valley.

Meanwhile, another party of volunteers followed a trail into the high country where they found a small party of Yosemites. The Indians did not resist and were brought peacefully to the valley.

This search went on for days. Volunteers entered more small villages nearby on the valley floor, all recently deserted. No Indians were found but one decrepit old woman sitting in chaparral beside the trail. On being questioned by the interpreter, she said she told the others to leave her since she could not keep up on the mountain trails.

"The others," mused Savage when Boling told him about the woman. "So they are there, in the mountains." He pondered, looking up at the heights. "We will find them. But not now. Our stores are just about exhausted. We must return to Mariposa. We *will* come back, and when we do, they will beg us to take them to the reservation."

"Now why will they do that, Major? They don't seem to be very interested at the moment," said Doctor Bunnell. He had sidled over when he heard Savage talking with Boling.

Savage ignored him, turned to Boling. "Burn everything. Houses, food supplies, meeting house, sweat lodges, everything."

"My God, Major! Isn't that a bit extreme?" said Bunnell. "You'll find only dead Indians when you return."

Savage glared at Bunnell, turned to Boling. "Do it!"

The Major and Boling walked away in different directions, leaving Bunnell where he stood. The doctor shook his head, looked up at the heavens.

*****

Jason brushed his horse with a fistful of coarse grass. The horse's reins were tied to a low branch of a large oak beside their u-ma-cha. He watched Tahnee who knelt at the cooking fire.

She told him that he needed to watch her making acorn mush so he could prepare it next time. She smiled at his frown, told him to watch carefully as she explained what she was doing.

She poured acorn meal into a large cooking basket and partially filled it with water. Picking up hot stones from the fire with two long sticks, she placed the stones in the basket. The mush adhered to the hot rocks. She explained each move and looked up to be sure he was watching and listening.

When the cooking was finished, she removed the stones with the tongs and dropped them into another basket filled with cold water. The mush on the stones congealed. She peeled the congealed mush from the stones, held it up to show to Jason.

"Looks good," he said. "I'll finish here in a minute."

He stopped brushing, his hand on the horse's neck, when he saw two young volunteers walking toward the u-ma-cha, carrying torches. They stopped when they saw Jason, looked anxiously at each other.

"Why the torches?" Jason said.

"Uh, Mr. Savage's orders," said one.

"What orders?" Jason said.

"Burn everything."

"What!" Only at that instant did Jason realize that the thin pillars of smoke rising in the village were not from cooking fires, but from flames on the sides of u-ma-cha.

"Stay away from that u-ma-cha," said Jason.

"We got our orders." The volunteers stepped toward the u-ma-cha. One extended the torch toward the side of the dwelling.

Tahnee rushed the volunteer and wrested the torch from him. She thrust it at him, and he backed away. He glanced at Jason and saw his hand resting on his pistol in its holster.

"Mr. Savage ain't gonna like this," he said.

The two volunteers walked away, looking back over their shoulders at Jason and Tahnee. She still held the torch.

Jason turned to her, smiling. "You're one mean full-grown grizzly," he said. She didn't smile, still watching the retreating volunteers.

In ten minutes, the two men returned, following Major Savage. He stopped before Jason and Tahnee.

"Bishop, I've tried to tolerate you, but my patience has limits. I am in charge here, and you are becoming a real nuisance. Now step aside, and let these men do their job."

"Major, I hear you have given orders to burn everything the Yosemites own. That's the devil's own work, and if there is a God in heaven, you'll answer for it. But your order has nothing to do with me. This u-ma-cha is mine, and I'm not a Yosemite."

"Stand aside, Bishop, or I'll arrest you and drag you back to Mariposa." During this conversation, a half dozen other volunteers arrived, some with torches, and stood behind Savage.

Savage turned to the others. "Burn it." They moved to the u-ma-cha and lit it in a half dozen places. The dry bark smoldered and caught fire.

Jason and Tahnee rushed inside the smoking interior and pulled out their belongings and food baskets, dragging everything to a heap away from the u-ma-cha. They stood over their belongings, coughing, wiping their eyes running with tears from the smoke, watching the u-ma-cha being enveloped in flames.

Savage walked over to Jason and Tahnee. "We are returning to Mariposa now, but we will come back. Soon. We haven't finished here. Next time we will find the Yosemites and take them to the reservation." He pointed at Tahnee. "You will go with the others. Be ready." He pointed at Jason. "You were right. This has nothing to do with you. Stay out of it."

"Now *this* has everything to do with me, Savage. Tahnee is with me. She hasn't been with the Yosemites for almost three years. She is mine, and you have no power over me or her."

"We'll be back," said Savage. He turned and walked away, followed by the others.

Jason and Tahnee watched their u-ma-cha, their home, vanish in the flames.

At dusk, a week later, Jason and Tahnee sat at a fire circle inside a small u-ma-cha. They began building it the very day the battalion withdrew from the valley, leaving their home and the villages in ashes. Yosemites who had come down from the hills after seeing the battalion leave built more small u-ma-cha nearby. Cooking fires burned before or inside most of the dwellings. Two deer carcasses hung from oak boughs outside the new village. Slices of flesh had been cut from both.

Tahnee leaned against Jason. "You sure?"

"Yes, I am. I have intended talking with you about getting married." He put his arm around her shoulders and pulled her close. "I love you, Tahnee. I want to be with you all the time. Forever. Do you understand 'forever?'"

"I understand."

"Don't think that I'm doing this because of what's happening to us. We just need to marry now rather than later. Is that okay?"

"Yes, it is okay, if you really want it. I want it."

"Is there someone here who can perform the ceremony? Is that what you call it, a ceremony? What's involved?"

"Well, you supposed to pay for me by giving things to my father. Robes, skins, things like this. But you cannot do this now. Maybe you give him things later when we see him again." She turned aside. "If we see him again."

She turned back, smiled. "We tell medicine man we want to marry. He say 'okay,' and we are married."

"That's it?"

"Yes, Yosemite way easier than white way. Linda . . . remember Linda in Sacramento?" He nodded. "Linda take me to Christian wedding. So . . . so complicate! Everybody promise everything! They keep promises?"

He smiled. "Well, usually, but not always. Sometimes they decide that they don't really love each other, and they get divorced. Getting divorced also is complicated. Do you understand divorce?"

"Yes. Linda tell me. Getting divorce not complicate with Yosemite. Just say 'I no want be married to you,' and marriage is finish."

"Is there a medicine man in the village?"

"Somebody tell me a medicine man still in mountain. I will ask somebody to find him, ask him to come. He will come."

Jason leaned over, kissed her on a cheek. He stood, pulled her up. "Good. Let's go to bed. I'm tired."

They undressed and lay on the bed of hides and skins. He pushed her dress up and explored her body, caressing and squeezing, pulled her to him, kissed her lips, the tip of her nose, her eyes.

"Hey! You say you tired," she said playfully.

"I lied."

Afterwards, they lay on their backs, breathing heavily, content.

He turned on his side, facing her. "Tell me a story," he said. "Tell me a Yosemite love story."

"Mmm. A Yosemite love story." She frowned, pondering, staring upward into the darkness. "Okay. Long, long ago, people who live in Ah-wah-nee very happy, have plenty food. Deer, fish, acorns, seeds and fruits, everything they need. The young chief, To-tau-kon-nu-la, was wise and loved by all the people. One day, he see people coming into valley led by a pretty young woman. He welcome the woman and her people.

"She say, 'I am Tis-sa-ack. We hear of the good chief, To-tau-kon-nu-la, and his happy people. We come from our land in the south to see you and give you presents.' So they give the chief and his people gifts of baskets, skins and beads. She and her people very happy and stay many days. She stay in great stone mountain at head of valley. Chief To-tau-kon-nu-la like her sweetness and beauty so much, he ask her to stay and be his wife.

"But she say she can not and must return with her people to their home in the south. So they go away. A terrible loneliness and sorrow came to To-tau-kon-nu-la. He did not know what to do. He leave his people and go look for her. For long, long time. He forget to call on Great Spirit to send rain, so streams dry up, and fish and deer die, and wild fruits and acorn trees die.

"Great Spirit very angry with To-tau-kon-nu-la. Earth shake, and smoke and flame come to hills and valley. The great stone dome at head of valley where Tis-sa-ack live break, and half fall into valley. You know great dome I talk about?"

"Yes."

She patted him on top of his head. "Good." She looked up at the u-ma-cha peak where the thin spiral of smoke was sucked through the opening. "Soon Great Spirit have pity on Yosemite people. Peace come again to Ah-wah-nee. Rains come, trees green again, flowers bloom.

"To-tau-kon-nu-la never come back. People believe he happy now, go to El-o-win, happy land other side setting sun. And the pretty face of Tis-sa-ack show on the front of split dome. Her face still there. You see it?"

"No," he said softly, his eyes half closed. "You show me tomorrow." He pulled her to him, kissed her forehead.

Spring came early to Ah-wah-nee. Snow still lay deep in the high country, but the valley floor was mostly clear, and wildflowers colored the meadows. Branches of deciduous trees showed leaf buds, and conifers displayed new dark green needles.

Tahnee and Jason stood at an u-ma-cha at the edge of the village with a young man and woman. "Jason, this my friend, Awanata. We best friends, grow up together, do everything together. Awanata's name mean 'turtle.'" Jason smiled, nodded. Awanata ducked her head, looked at her companion.

"And this her husband, Tocho. He Paiute, from other side of mountains where sun rise. He come to Ah-wah-nee two year ago, then go to gold streams in foothills. He work there with other Indians more than one year until white miners tell all Indian miners to go. Tocho angry and fight them—his name mean 'mountain lion.'" Tocho smiled. "But they have guns, so he leave. He speak good English, better than me."

In the days following, the village grew as more Yosemites came down from the high country where they had fled from the volunteers. Some built u-ma-cha, others moved in with relatives who had returned before them. The village took on a settled look. Men brought in deer carcasses they hung from tree limbs. Women prepared hides for clothing and bags. Children scampered about the village, shouting and laughing. Some played hide-and-seek. Others collected and threw stems of the rattlesnake weed at each other, the seeds adhering to clothing and hair.

Tahnee and Awanata worked together, grinding acorns, preparing meals, cooking, smiling and talking, excited and enthusiastic about whatever they happened to be doing. Jason often listened to their chatter, smiling, until Tahnee told him to go away. You bother me, she said. She smiled, reluctantly.

Jason and Tocho hunted and fished together. Tocho indeed spoke rather good English, mimicking the rough language he had learned among white miners, but he also spoke the Yosemite language he had learned from Awanata and the villagers. Jason took the opportunity to try to pick up words and phrases in the Yosemite tongue from him.

Jason had made no attempt to learn the Yosemite language from Tahnee, content to speak English with her. Now he surprised her occasionally with a new expression that he had learned from Tocho. Each time he said something in Yosemite, she congratulated him, and then they laughed at his pronunciation or misuse of a word. He was not offended. He would bear anything to see her happy.

Yet, on one occasion, sitting on the ground in front of the u-ma-cha, she laughed too hard, and he frowned. She sobered. "I sorry, Jason. Remember Tocho is Paiute. He learn Yosemite from Awanata, and he does not speak Yosemite very good. So you learn bad Yosemite from Tocho. I teach you my language."

"Suits me fine, little grizzly."

They looked up at a shout. Two Yosemite men ran in the meadow toward the village, shouting and pointing at the western slopes. When they arrived, they stopped and gasped, catching their breath, as villagers crowded around them. The men spoke excitedly, gesturing westward, and spoke rapidly to the villagers.

"What's going on?" Jason said. "Is it the battalion?"

"Yes," Tahnee said. "These two men hunt in forest above valley. They see many white riders coming up mountain on other side. They say the riders will be here tonight or tomorrow morning."

As Tahnee explained to Jason, villagers scattered, running to their u-ma-cha. There they gathered clothing, blankets, threw food into baskets. Their arms full, they ran toward the mountain. Everyone knew why the battalion had returned.

*****

Jason and Tahnee watched Captain Boling and two dozen volunteers ride into the village. In the distance, a larger force rode slowly from the trees into the meadow. Boling's force pulled up, and he dismounted.

Boling looked around, spoke to Jason. "Why didn't you run with the others?"

"I'm not a Yosemite."

"She is."

"She's my wife."

"The major said she would have to move with the others to the reservation."

"Are you going to tell the Major that his five Indian wives must move to the reservation?"

Boling looked aside, grimacing, then back at Jason. "You know as well as I that his wives are not Yosemites and, anyway, that has nothing to do with what we're about here." He turned to his troop, still mounted.

"Lt. Gilbert, ride to the base of the hills. Tracks should lead you to the trails they took up the hillsides. Find them, and bring them down under guard. If they resist, you know the orders." The volunteers rode off.

"The orders are to kill them?" said Jason to Boling.

Boling mounted, looked up at the mountain, then back to Jason. "Bishop, this is more complicated than you realize. We're under orders from the State of California. We're doing what we must, what is best for the people of California."

"What about the Yosemite people? They lived here before the white people came, before the Spanish came."

Boling exhaled deeply, shook his head. "I'll be back." He pointed at Tahnee. "You be ready." He turned to Jason. "If you know what's good for her and you, you'll stay out of this. If you want to ride down with us, you're welcome as long as you don't interfere. If you interfere, you'll be considered a hostile."

"And you shoot hostiles."

Boling glared at Jason, swung his horse around and rode after the troop.

Jason and Tahnee were alone, watching the volunteers riding from the village toward the hills.

"He intends to take you . . . us . . . by force," Jason said. "We must leave before they return."

"Go with us." They turned to see Tocho at his u-ma-cha entrance. Awanata came out and stood beside him. They had been hiding inside, listening. "We will go to my people across the mountain," said Tocho. "The battalion will not go there. Both of us have Ahwahneechee wives. If we stay, we will lose them."

Jason looked at Tahnee. She nodded. "We will go with you," said Jason. "We should leave now. They could come back any time. We'll pack the horses and walk."

"I think the trail too hard for horses," said Tocho. "Too steep, too much rock."

"We'll take them as far as we can."

The two couples went to their u-ma-cha and quickly gathered belongings and food baskets. Jason strapped on his pistol belt and shouldered the Leman. He went to the rough pen where the horses were kept, brought them to the u-ma-cha where he and Tocho tied baskets and blankets on their backs.

At the muffled sounds of gunshots, all four looked abruptly toward the slopes on the northern side of the valley.

"We must go," Jason said. "Everyone ready?" They nodded.

While Jason and Tocho checked the burdens tied on the horses' backs, Tahnee and Awanata stood quietly, looking about at the deserted village. Tahnee glanced up at the split dome, the forests at the base of the cliffs, the meadow that stretched westward to wooded slopes above the foot of the valley. She turned to Awanata, and both wiped tears with sleeves.

Jason encircled Tahnee's shoulders with an arm. "You'll come back some day," he said softly. She leaned on his shoulder.

The four set out toward the head of the valley, toward the stone mountain with the split dome, Jason and Tocho each leading a horse carrying all the belongings that now represented home for each couple.

# Chapter 16

The four companions climbed the steep path above the valley, making their way on switchbacks to ease the climb for the horses. At the distant sound of gunfire, they stopped, listened. Single scattered shots, then volleys. They looked at each other, grim.

"They are killing my people," Tahnee said. "What can we do?"

"We need to keep moving," said Jason. He took her arm and stepped around a boulder in the trail. She walked up beside Awanata. He looked back at Tocho who had stopped a few yards back and was adjusting his horse's pack.

"Hey! You up there!"

Jason and the others started, looked down the back trail. A half dozen volunteers crouched behind boulders, rifles held at the ready. The speaker stood in the trail. "Come down now!" He beckoned them to come.

Tocho, wide-eyed, gripped the reins of his horse that had shied at the shout from below. A shot cracked, and Tocho was blown against the horse. The horse galloped into the forest, and Tocho fell to the ground, blood oozing from the hole in his back.

The leader's remark to his men was almost inaudible. "Goddammit, I told you to wait for my order." He stepped behind a boulder.

"Behind rocks!" shouted Jason. He dropped his reins, ran to the women, pushed them behind a large boulder, and shucked the rifle from his shoulder. He dropped behind another boulder nearby.

A shout from below: "Are you coming down?"

"I'm an American!" shouted Jason from behind his boulder. "Leave me be!"

"You're shielding hostiles!" from below. "Hands in the air, all of you, and come on down!"

Jason waited.

His silence was answered by shots from below that struck his sheltering boulder in rapid succession, sending stone chips flying in all directions. Jason peered around the side of the boulder, saw glimpses of the shooters and fired at them. One man fell from his cover into the trail. Angry shouts came from below.

Jason turned and spoke to the rock that sheltered Tahnee and Awanata. "I'm going to fire a number of shots as quickly as I can. When you hear this, run. Run uphill, behind cover if you can."

"No, I stay with you!" said Tahnee.

"Go! I'll find you!"

Shots from below peppered Jason's boulder. He pulled his pistol from the holster, set it on the ground beside him. He raised the rifle, spoke over his shoulder. "When you hear me shoot, run!" He peered around the boulder, fired the rifle, picked up the pistol and fired. A grunt was heard from below, followed by cursing.

The shots from below ceased, then a lone shot, a pause, then another shot. After a long pause, a shout: "We'll get you, you son-of a-bitch, goddamed Indian-lover!" Then nothing but silence.

Jason waited. He looked up at the rock that had sheltered Tahnee and Awanata. "Tahnee," he said softly. He listened. No response came but the sound of wind in the canopy.

Reloading the rifle and pistol, he leaned on the bounder. He waited for what seemed days, until the bright sky was replaced by gray dusk, and the treetops disappeared in the twilight.

He glanced anxiously down the trail. Seeing no movement, he stood slowly, looked down where the volunteers had hidden, then looked uphill. Nothing moved in his view. He pushed the pistol into its holster and shouldered the rifle.

Stepping cautiously from behind the boulder, he looked below and saw the darkness in the trail that was Tocho's body. He closed his eyes, regretted that he could not bury him, but there was no time. He climbed up the trail to the boulder where Tahnee and Awanata had taken cover. They had left no trace.

He searched the dark forest where his horse had bolted, but found no sign of his mount or Tocho's. There were no prints in the thick layer of dry leaves and needles. Returning to the trail, he climbed slowly upward, looking right and left for any sign of the fleeing women. He saw nothing and dared not call. Not yet.

Continuing to climb, he searched until darkness forced him to find a stopping place. He sat down, exhausted, shivering, fumbled in his coat pocket and found the two sticks that a Chickasaw gave him when he was a boy.

The old Indian had showed him how to make fire with the sticks and tinder and applauded him when he struck his first flame. Jason had carried the two sticks ever since as a sort of talisman. Over the years, he had occasionally made fire with the sticks, more for nostalgia than necessity. His present circumstance suggested necessity.

After scooping out a fire pit, he collected a few handfuls of dry grass and twigs and started a fire after considerable exertion and a litany of prayers and curses. He stared into the flames, added dry sticks and watched them ignite. Forcing himself to stand, he stumbled about, collecting sticks and dry boughs, dropping them in a stack beside the fire.

Sitting down heavily, he added wood to the fire and warmed his hands, staring into the flames. He looked up at the dark sky, only a hint of a moon showing through the gloom, felt the cold wind on his cheeks. He pulled his jacket collar up and his hat down, hunching his shoulders. Nodding, he closed his eyes, opened his eyes wide and rubbed his face with both hands. Nodding, his eyes closed, and he lay down, just for a minute, he said to himself. Must stay awake, he mumbled aloud.

"Gotcha."

Jason opened his eyes, looked up to see a pistol pointing at his head. He sat up slowly, rubbing his eyes. Last evening, he had planned to keep the fire built up and stay awake all night. He figured he could sleep hidden during the day when he needed to. He had been more worn out than he thought. Now the fire was cold, half of a bright sun ball was visible on the eastern horizon, and he stared into the receiving end of a pistol.

"Move real slow," said the volunteer who held the pistol. Another volunteer stood nearby, rubbing the sleep from his eyes. "We got some riding to do. We even got a horse for you. Found him just a few minutes ago eatin' grass over there and a load of goods strapped on his back. Looks like somebody planned to take a trip some place." He grinned.

Jason looked at the three horses. Sure enough, one was his horse tied to the same limb with two others, and the packs were still intact.

"Buddy, get rid of them packs." He kept the pistol pointed at Jason's head. "We're gonna turn that packhorse into a ridin' horse." He turned to Jason. "Hope you can ride bareback, for if you cain't, you got a long walk ahead of ya.'"

Buddy yawned, pulled a knife from a belt scabbard and cut the packs from the horse. The packs tumbled to the ground, spilling their contents.

"Buddy, you take the lead, and our guest here will follow you. I'll bring up the rear." He raised the pistol toward Jason. "And I'll shoot you down if you make me mad. I thank it was you that shot two of our boys down the hill. The Captain said we were to bring you back alive, but I might have to shoot you when you try to get away."

Buddy laughed. "Harley, you mean you're gonna shoot him and tell Boling that he tried—"

"Shut up. Just git the horses, git mounted, and lead off."

Buddy nodded, looked at the ground, spoke under his breath. "Okay, just sayin.'" He untied the three horses, walked over and handed reins to Harley and Jason. Buddy mounted and moved off. Harley mounted and waited as Jason gripped fistfuls of his horse's mane and struggled to mount. That done, he fell in behind buddy, Harley following.

The sun was high when Jason rode between his two captors into the battalion bivouac at the foot of the valley. Volunteers were busy breaking camp, but most stopped what they were doing to watch the three coming.

"Who's that? What's he doin' here?" said a volunteer to no one in particular as the riders passed. No one answered.

The three rode by a knot of Yosemites that huddled together at the edge of the encampment, sorting and tying up bundles of clothing and food baskets. Some whispered to each other as they rode by.

The three pulled up where volunteers were taking down Captain Boling's tent. Boling and Doctor Bunnell stood silently nearby. They watched the three riders dismount.

"Found him at the top of that trail that goes up to the lake," said Harley. "I thank he's the one that shot our two boys."

"That right?" said Boling to Jason.

"If you mean did I try to protect myself from being gunned down by a bunch of men who were trying to kill me, then, yeah, I did shoot back."

Boling stared at Jason a long moment, turned to Harley. "Get him something to eat. You're in charge of him. Harley, is it?"

"Yes, sir. Here's his pistol belt and rifle." Harley handed the guns to Boling. Harley and Jason walked away, leading their horses while Buddy walked in another direction.

Boling and Bunnell watched Harley and Jason. Bunnell turned to Boling. "What are you going to do with him?"

"Don't know. I'll let the Major decide. Officially, he's a hostile."

"He's not an Indian, so he hardly fits the definition."

"He fired on our men and might have killed some."

"He was shooting back at men who probably fired on him first. Self-defense."

"Damn it, Bunnell, this is not a shootout in the street in front of a saloon. It's a lawful operation, and he's on the wrong side. He was trying to prevent us taking his wife, a Yosemite, along with the other Yosemites, to the reservation."

"I see. So he and his wife were living here peacefully in this valley, where her people have lived for at least a few centuries, and when some outsiders come in here to try to force her to go somewhere else, he tried to prevent that. He was trying to protect his wife, just like Major Savage would try to protect his Indian wives if somebody wanted to take them from him and force them to live elsewhere."

"Don't you start on that, Bunnell. You tend to your doctoring, and I'll tend to what this expedition is all about." Boling walked away, carrying Jason's pistol belt and rifle. "God, I hate this," he mumbled.

Battalion members rode slowly down the main trail toward the valley, through pine forests and scattered stands of oak and fir and cedar. The Yosemites walked silently in the midst of the riders.

Jason walked with the Indians, leading his horse. Harley rode behind Jason, shaking his head. More than once, he had told Jason to "git on your horse," and Jason had ignored him.

In the battalion's evening camps, Jason often sat with Harley, his captor, guide, and, eventually, confidant.

Harley, it seems, was a loner. Unlucky in panning for gold in the northern streams, he had cowboyed briefly on a ranch near Stockton, then drifted to Mariposa where he worked in the livery. He got caught up in the battalion, he said, for something to do more exciting than brushing horses and mucking out stalls.

Jason contributed little to the conversation. He simply listened to Harley while his mind raced. He could think of nothing but what had become of Tahnee.

Where had she and Awanata gone? Had they made it to Tocho's village? He remembered that Awanata said that she had visited the village with Tocho a year or so ago, so she might be able to find her way there again. She could not speak the Paiute language, but maybe Tahnee could find someone who spoke English. Maybe . . . maybe . . .

Harley was opening himself up so much in their conversations that Jason figured that Harley was unconsciously looking for a friend, someone he could rely on. Someone he could trust.

Jason began to ponder whether he could benefit from Harley's state of mind. At the beginning of the ride down from Ah-wah-nee, Harley was always with Jason. But now, they were sometimes apart, only for a moment, when one of them was behind a bush, or another was hobbling his horse.

One evening, while cooking fires were being built, Jason and Harley walked out of camp to collect firewood. Jason turned casually away from Harley, stooping to pick up sticks, moving gradually away, glancing back at Harley, moving away until he stepped out of sight into a heavy birch copse. He dropped the sticks and quickened his pace through the copse, pushing branches aside, looking over his shoulder, walking briskly until he emerged from the copse. And almost collided with Harley.

"We was out collecting firewood," Harley said. "Where's your firewood?" His hand rested on the pistol at his belt. "I've enjoyed our talks, Jason, but I'm in charge of you. Don't make me do what I gotta do if you try to get away." He was not smiling. "Now let's get back to camp. Maybe we can collect a little firewood on the way."

"I don't know why you're doing this, Mister Bunnell, but I sure do appreciate it."

Jason and Doctor Bunnell stood in darkness in a thick grove of oaks looking down on the battalion's camp. The embers of evening cooking fires glowed in the distance. Jason finished saddling his horse, slid the rifle into its bucket. He wore his pistol belt.

"There's not much I can do to show I don't support this godawful stupid operation," said Bunnell, "but I can do this."

"Hope this doesn't get you in hot water with the Captain."

"Oh, he'll decide that you found some means to get away. Besides, Boling isn't too happy with the whole affair himself. He's a good soldier and does what he's told, but the more he is faced with the fate of these people, the more he regrets his part in it. He'll send out patrols to look for you, but I wager he'll hope they don't find you."

"I feel bad about Harley. Savage is going to crucify him."

Bunnell smiled. "Well, maybe not. The whole camp had a little celebration this evening sort of marking the end of this affair. Most of the volunteers got a snoot full. I offered some of the boys, a bunch that included Harley, a bottle of my best brandy. I suspect most of them didn't even make it to their bedrolls.

"Now, you must be off before the camp stirs. Get as far away as you can, as quickly as possible. Boling won't send out patrols until sunup, and he won't have them out long. Everybody is anxious to get home."

Jason extended his hand, and Bunnell took it.

"Good luck," said Bunnell.

Jason swung up on his horse and rode at a walk up the slope, above the trail. He raised his arm in a salute, still facing forward, and disappeared into the dark forest.

The sun was high before Jason stopped. He had ridden toward the sun ball since it first cleared the eastern horizon, and now it was overhead. He figured he would head for the high country above Ah-wah-nee. That's where Tahnee and Awanata should be.

After riding until mid-afternoon, he dismounted on a prominence that commanded a clear view of miles in all directions. He saw only trees, rocky pinnacles, shaded, grassy forest glades. No movement but a large eagle overhead, almost stationary in the invisible updraft.

*Where are you, Tahnee?*

He rode for days in the high country, searching. The small bag of food Doctor Bunnell had given him was long gone, and he subsisted now on berries and the occasional small game he was able to shoot, usually squirrels. After days of eating nothing but roots and berries, he killed a fox and feasted on the charred flesh.

Riding the northern rim on the heights above Ah-wah-nee, he dismounted at a cliff edge and peered down at the distant floor. He saw no movement, nor any sign of habitation but the faint black ash stains of what had been the last Yosemite village, his and Tahnee's home.

*Where are you, Tahnee?*

Jason rode eastward through forest-covered granite canyons, higher and higher until forests gave way to stony hillsides and tall peaks wearing mantles of snow. He crossed the spine of the mountains and descended once again to forests of aspen, cottonwoods and lodgepole pine.

He stood now at the edge of a village in late afternoon, holding his horse's reins. He faced four warriors, three with bows in hand, arrows notched. The fourth held a club. Jason spoke to them in English. They looked at each other, bewildered.

"Tocho," Jason said, "Paiute. Numa." Tocho had told him the name his people called themselves.

The Indians smiled, lowered their bows. "Ah, ah, Numa," said one who touched his chest and beckoned him to come. Jason followed them into the village of cone-shaped huts fashioned from bundles of long grasses or mats woven from tule reeds. One of the warriors talked with an old man who looked at Jason as they talked. He walked to Jason.

"You look for someone? Tocho?" the man said in English.

Jason sighed, smiled. "You speak English. Tocho was my Paiute friend at Ah-wah-nee. Tocho was killed by Americans. I look for Tocho's Ahwahneechee wife, Awanata, and my Ahwahneechee wife, Tah-nee-hay. I thought they might have come here when the whites came to Ah-wah-nee."

The man talked with the warriors who had confronted Jason and now listened eagerly. They talked with each other and shook their heads.

"Nobody know Tocho. Nobody see Ahwahneechee wives."

Jason closed his eyes, lowered his head.

"You stay here in village. I send men other villages, ask if they know Tocho, see Awahneechee women."

"Thank you for your help. You are very kind. Thank you."

Jason followed the man through the village, leading his horse and nodding to people who stopped what they were doing to stare at this stranger, likely the first white man many had seen. Children watched, wide-eyed, as he passed, smiling at them. They moved behind a parent as they watched the horse pass.

The old man stopped at a grass hut. "You stay here. I send men now." He walked away.

Jason led his horse to a small pond behind the village. After the horse had drunk, Jason took him to a patch of grass and hobbled him. He removed the saddle and blanket and bridle and carried them to the hut. Stowing the gear inside, he sat on a log beside the hut, exhaled deeply and looked around.

Their curiosity satisfied that this stranger was neither a threat nor worth more of their time, the villagers returned to their usual routine. Jason watched, exhausted, his mind blank. The women at their huts worked at scraping hides and sewing, tending children, drying meat. Some of the women wore a skin apron, others an apron fashioned from a fiber of bark or reeds. A number of women wore full-length dresses of fringed hide. The few men in camp wore a skin breechclout, some with a fringed buckskin shirt and leggings. Men and women wore moccasins of animal skin, some ankle high, or sandals of woven yucca or sagebrush bark.

Sounds were muted, children playing, a mother's soft admonition, a breeze whispering in the pines at the edge of the village. At the approach of night, even these slight sounds and movements diminished until the village was quiet, seemingly deserted.

Jason looked up in the gloaming at the approach of a woman. She dumped a load of firewood and moss beside the fire circle and handed him a small wooden bowl of piñon nuts, seeds and berries. He smiled and nodded his thanks. A hint of a smile played about her lips. He watched as she laid tinder and sticks on the ashes in the fire circle. She went to a nearby hut, took a burning stick from the fire there and lit Jason's fire. She stood and left as if these were tasks she did each day.

Jason slept fitfully that night near the entrance of the straw hut, waking a number of times to stoke the fire outside the entrance. Each time he went back inside and lay down, he dropped off quickly but hardly slept, rolling and perspiring in spite of the cold.

He rose at first light, heavy from lack of sleep, his head aching. He went outside, added sticks to the embers, sat down to wait and try to settle the raging turmoil in his head.

The man he had talked with the previous day, who seemed to be a chief or headman of sorts, with a half dozen men following, walked up to him. He stood and greeted them with a raised hand.

The headman raised a hand in reply. "The men I send to other villages come back during night. No one has seen the women you seek."

Jason drooped, his head down. He recovered. "Thank you for trying. I must look elsewhere. Now I will go. Thank you."

Reaching inside the hut, he dragged saddle, bridle and blanket outside, hefted them unsteadily. He walked to his horse, wobbling, already exhausted. He bridled and saddled the horse while the men watched. Mounting, he waved a goodbye and pointed his horse westward, back up the mountain. But where to look?

*Where are you, Tahnee? Why is this happening? Again.*

The ride from the Paiute village up the eastern slopes to the frigid spine of the range, then down the western side was like a dream, his mind wandering, hardly seeing long stretches of the trail, dozing, his mind racing, recovering to pull the horse back on the trail. The nights were hardly a respite, sleeping fitfully, shivering, feeding a fire that did not warm.

On a day that began too early, he crossed a rocky flat, dozing and almost falling from his horse. He awakened abruptly to find his mount stopped at the edge of a precipice that looked out over a wide, deep valley. He blinked and looked below. Ah-wah-nee.

He rode slowly down the rocky switchback trail that led from the heights to the valley floor. At the top, in his stupor, he had not even thought about the possibility that she might be here, but now, nearing the valley . . . Maybe they came back.

*Are you here, Tahnee?*

His hopes disappeared in the light breeze that blew across the valley floor. The village was but a memory, a thin black dry sheet on the plain. Puffs of wind lifted flakes of ash, swirling, rising and vanishing. Soon even these reminders of the village would be gone.

He looked up, and tears clouded his view. He squeezed his eyes shut, opened them and saw the split dome at the head of the valley.

*Tahnee, you said that Tis-sa-ack lived in the half dome. You said you would show me her image, and I never let you show it to me. Tahnee, is she there yet? Are you with her?*

He dropped to his knees, exhausted in body and mind, lowered his head, eyes closed, sobbing.

After a moment, he stood, looked at the heavens, shook his head. "Ah, man, get a hold of yourself!" he said aloud. Wiping his eyes with a sleeve, he looked around. He walked to his horse, nibbling on a patch of grass, reins trailing.

Grass. He looked around. Tiny green shoots showed all over the plain, evidence that the natural beauty of the valley would recover, but there would be no one here to enjoy it.

His dark mood deepened as he mounted and rode toward the switchback trail where he had last seen Tahnee and Awanata. Maybe he missed something when he went this way before, searching in haste, thinking he would easily find them.

He dismounted and led his horse up the trail, winced when he saw the dark remains that had been Tocho, now ravaged by scavengers and insects, rib bones exposed and eye sockets empty. He kicked leaves and detritus over the body, almost heaved when he accidentally nudged the skull, separating it from the body.

He shuddered and climbed higher on the trail, stopping a moment where Tahnee and Awanata had taken cover behind the boulder, then continued to the plateau above and eastward, investigating the various routes that the two women might have taken.

After days of agonizing search, he decided that the journey across the high passes would be too much for two women on foot, with no food supplies, blankets and coats. He turned westward. Maybe they had headed for the low country on the western slopes. The Ahwahneechee had hunted and gathered extensively there. They would know this country. Tahnee and Awanata would want to escape the cold. They would go to the warmer foothills.

*That's where I will find them!* He rode across the pass west of Ah-wah-nee and down the same trail they had ridden up from the central valley. He was anxious now, expectant. His mind cleared, his hunger forgotten. He resisted the impulse to push his horse into a gallop down the twisting, stony trail.

He decided that the two women would not stay on this main trail since it would be used by riders that surely would be going to see Ah-wah-nee, this earthly paradise, now that it was known. He searched the slopes on each side of the main trail for alternate paths. He was unsure what he looked for. Footprints could be left by anyone. The women likely could not make fire, so there would be no abandoned fire pits. Could they even have survived this long? He refused to accept that he would not find them. They must be here. Somewhere.

*Where are you, Tahnee?*

*****

He searched for any sign, from dawn to sunset, criss-crossing trails, across grassy vales, through dense forests, down into and across rocky ravines. He slept fitfully beside the fire, tormented by dreams of conflagrations and screams, the explosions of gunfire. He woke often, perspiring yet shivering. He threw more sticks on the fire and dropped off again, wrestling with his demons.

By habit, he cared for his horse, finding grass and streams, but he neglected to care for himself. He ate little more than berries and roots. He found old acorns and chewed on them, but retched after swallowing the bitter nuts. His ammunition was gone, so he had no meat. Once he lay on the bank of a shallow stream and caught a small trout with his hands. Ravenous, he ate it raw, biting off chunks of the cold flesh.

He awoke one morning, his fire dead, to find his horse gone. The hobbles were where he had left them last evening, on the ground beside the saddle, set out for hobbling, forgotten. He clenched his eyes, determined that he would not break down.

He wandered aimlessly. He had lost track of place and time, but not purpose. He scavenged for berries, dug with his hands for roots, finding little edible. Almost delirious from hunger and despair, he was beset day and night by images of firestorms, screaming people, gunshots.

On a steep slope, he struggled upward blindly through tangled underbrush, his vision blurred. He fell to hands and knees, exhausted. His head hung, mouth open, gasping.

*Is this where it ends?* He shook his head, uttered an anguished cry and struggled to stand. He weaved, straightened and pushed through the underbrush into the open.

And then he was there. He shook his head, clenched his eyes and wiped them with a sleeve, trying to clear his vision. It was the u-ma-cha. He shook his head again.

*Is this a dream. Maybe I really am mad.*

He squeezed his eyes again, opened them. It was the u-ma-cha. And Tahnee stood there at the entrance. He was paralyzed, fearful. He clenched his eyes, shook his head. He opened his eyes. She was still there, looking at him.

"Tahnee!" He staggered up the slope, stumbled and fell, struggled up and was enveloped in Tahnee's arms. He threw his arms around her shoulders and pulled her gently to him, tears wetting his cheeks.

He leaned back. "Tahnee," he said softly. "I thought I had lost you again. I—"

"Where you been? I wait for you long time." She feigned an angry look, then softened when she saw the hurt on his face. She touched his cheek, wiped his tears. "You look like old man. You hungry?"

He pulled her to him and held her, resting his cheek on her head. "Yes, Tahnee, sweetheart, I feel like an old man, an old man who has just been reborn." He leaned back, kissed her lips lightly.

"Yes, I am hungry. If you don't give me something to eat right now, I'm going to eat you up." He reached for her. "First this wing, then this haunch," squeezing her arm, then her butt, "and this drumstick," reaching for her leg. She laughed, fended him off, jumping backwards. He stopped, gasped, looked up at the blue cloudless sky. He stretched out his arms, smiling.

"I've died and gone to heaven."

They sat at a fire before the u-ma-cha entrance. Jason tore pieces of flesh from a rabbit that Tahnee had roasted over the flames. He turned the carcass over and over, stripping the last slivers. After sucking on the bones, he tossed the bare skeleton into the flames.

"How do you do it? Rabbits and squirrels, I'm surprised you don't have a deer hanging in a tree."

"I make little snares from vines and my hair and pieces my deerskin dress. Easy. I make fishhook too. I catch fish tomorrow." She cocked her head, smiled impishly.

"You are a wonder, my little full-grown female grizzly Ahwahneechee sweetheart." He leaned over, kissed her cheek. "Now. Tell me."

"Okay. When you tell us to run when you start shooting, we get ready. When you shoot, we jump up, run into trees up hill. At top, we so tired, we fall to ground to rest. We get up, walk many, many miles toward high mountain. Awanata think she can find way to Tocho's village. We try sleep together, hug for warm, but no sleep. Too cold. We shake all night.

"Next day, we walk before sun come up. We climb steep hill. Then we hear men behind, down trail, yell 'stop!' We so afraid. We run. I run off to side, down rocky hillside. Awanata try run straight up hill, but too steep. She slide and fall. Men come closer, shoot her. They cannot come after me. Hill too steep for horses.

"I hide behind big rock. I hear man yell, 'we'll get you!' I wait long time until they go away. I climb to see Awanata. I cry, Jason. She dead, already cold. I want to bury her or burn her body, but I cannot. I put rocks on her body, but I not find enough to cover her. I so sad. Now she and Tocho are together in El-o-win other side of setting sun."

Jason held her as she cried softly.

She wiped her tears with a hand. "I wonder what to do. I think of going to Ah-wah-nee. I walk toward my valley, but I hear shots in distance, maybe from valley. I think, maybe you are killed. Then I say, *no*, you will not be killed! I will see you again, and we will live together for all time, like you say." She took his arm and leaned on his shoulder, wiped a tear from her cheek.

"I walk about, not know where to go. I look many days for other Ahwahneechee, but see no one. I decide I will go to only place where I was free and happy for long time. Our u-ma-cha. Now I here. Now you here." She reached up and kissed his cheek.

"This is our place, Tahnee. I wish we could stay here forever. But we cannot. You know that." She looked into the fire, nodded, laid her head on his shoulder.

"Now you tell me," she said.

He put an arm over her shoulders and pulled her close, looked into the embers. "When the shooting stopped, I looked behind your boulder . . ."

Jason and Tahnee lay on their stomachs on a hillock at sunset, looking over the top at distant Mariposa. Lights flickered on like fireflies as lanterns were lit in kitchens and sitting rooms and saloons.

Jason rolled over on his back, and Tahnee followed. He clasped his hands on his chest, looked up at a lacy cloud layer, the soft red color fading gradually to a hint of pink, then disappearing in a gray sky that became night. The overcast lifted, and landscape forms reappeared as outlines under a weak moon.

Jason rolled over again and looked back at the town. Tahnee rolled over and laid her hand on his shoulder. He looked at her and smiled. "Now we wait," he said.

Jason stood and stretched. "Soon," he said. They watched the lights in Mariposa disappear one by one as lamps were extinguished, signaling bedtime for most, and closing time for some. Soon all lights had disappeared but for a few that Jason figured would remain lit all night. He reached down, took Tahnee's hand, helped her stand. She stretched and yawned.

"It's not the last time we'll sleep on the ground, but the next time we'll have warm blankets and a fire."

"Okay, you say so."

They hefted small packs and walked toward the town, staying in shadows and scrub off the main trails. At the edge of town, they walked around behind the row of shops and the Outpost, past the livery. Passing a house with a light in a back bedroom, they bent and crept behind chaparral.

They stopped in the backyard of Bess and Billy's place. A dim light shone at the side, probably from the dining room. Jason pondered. He took Tahnee's arm, and they walked to the house, stepped up on the back porch.

He knocked gently. Nothing. He knocked just a bit harder, winced at the sound, hoping no one but someone inside the house heard. He waited, looked at

Tahnee, uncertain. He leaned forward, his face almost touching the door. He knocked again. "Bess," he said softly.

Someone heard. From the other side of the door, the stern sound of Bess's voice: "There's a big shotgun with both barrels loaded pointed at your chest through this door. If you turn around, slowly, you'll see my old man has a pistol pointed at your head."

Jason turned slowly and saw Billy five steps away, clearly visible in the moonlight, with a pistol aimed at his head.

"Billy, it's Jason and Tahnee," Jason said softly.

The pistol lowered, and Billy stepped up, grinning broadly. He leaned his head against the door. "Open up, Bess. It's friends."

The door opened. There stood Bess, frowning, holding the shotgun at the ready, outlined from the lantern behind her in the dining room. She saw Tahnee.

"Land sakes! Git in here!" She grabbed Tahnee with one arm, squeezing her tightly, the other hand holding the shotgun at her side. Billy ushered Jason inside, shut and locked the door.

Bess held up a hand to stop the three from walking further. She went into the dining room and pulled curtains over windows. She came back to the hall. "Now you come in and sit down. I'll make some coffee." When they stepped into the light of the dining room, she frowned, looked them up and down. "Lordy, you two look like you hadn't eat in months. You want something to eat?"

"Coffee will be much appreciated," Jason said. "We'll be fine till breakfast. If you'll have us for breakfast."

She mock-frowned and hustled for the kitchen. She stopped in the doorway and turned back. "Take your same room. There's nobody here now, just me and the old man."

The three sat down while Billy brought them up to date on what had been happening recently in Mariposa. The battalion had returned after the second march to Yosemite, bringing a few Ahwahneechee who had been sent on to the reservation. Major Savage had proclaimed the removal of the mountain Indians a success and disbanded the battalion.

"I thank everone was real glad it was over," Billy said. "A lot of the volunteers had decided that this was a sorry thing to do, burning people's homes and things and making them move away from their country. Course, a lot of the boys thought it was a great idea and lots of fun, and they was real happy they had done the thing." He looked at Tahnee. "Sorry, missy." Tahnee put her hand on Billy's, smiled, a tired smile.

Bess brought a tray holding four mugs of steaming coffee, a plate of biscuits and a jar of red jam and a couple of knives. She set everything on the table, leaned back, hands on hips. "Lordy, you two are a mess." She sniffed. "Like you been rolling in a pig pen. Well, knowing you, there has to be a reason." She smiled. "We'll take care of all that, we will." She sat down. "Now eat something." Each took a mug and sipped.

Jason and Tahnee took biscuits. Jason slathered his with jam and put half in his mouth. He chewed, eyes closed. "Um-*umm.* Bess, I read a book one time that talked about ambrosia, food for the gods. This biscuit and jam is ambrosia." He took another biscuit.

"Glad you like it," she said. "Now, what's going on?"

Jason set his mug on the table. “I’m going to tell you everything that’s happened to us since we last saw you, but first, I’m going to ask a big favor. We need animals, gear and supplies to get us on our way. Two riding horses and tack, another horse or mule for packing, a small tent, camp gear and supplies. I’ll need a rifle and ammunition for the rifle and pistol. If you don’t want to get involved, I will understand and no hard feelings.”

“Git off, Jason,” said Billy. “You know we’ll do anything we can for you. We’ll git everthing you need. If anybody asks questions about what I’m doing, I’ll lie. I lie pretty good.” He smiled at Bess. “Maybe I’ll tell ’em we’re laying in stuff for a hunt or visiting kinfolk down south. I still have kin where I come from. Anyway, I been in this town before it was a town. I can do anything I want, and nobody is going to bother me. If they do, I’ll knock ’em down.”

“He will,” said Bess, “and I’ll help ’im.”

“You’re a couple of angels,” Jason said, “and that’s for sure.”

“We’ll git on it tomorrow,” said Bess. “I expect you’re in a hurry. We might be able to finish tomorrow, but more likely it’ll take a couple of days to git the stuff together. You stay inside and out of sight. Nobody will be coming in. The place is closed for cleaning, you know.” She smiled.

As Bess predicted, it required two days to accumulate the animals and gear and supplies they needed. Billy had no problem with the horses. He regularly dealt with a man who had a horse ranch south of town. The rancher always had animals for sale to supply the growing population of the Mariposa area.

Bess adopted the ruse of an extended trip down south to visit Billy's kin to explain her purchases. When one shopkeeper asked why she needed so much camp cooking gear, she explained that she was replacing old gear they hadn't used in years. Food purchases, she said, were both for the guesthouse and the trip south.

In the dark hours before sunrise of the second night, Billy brought the saddled riding horses and packhorse from the livery and tied the reins to the rail at the back door. While Bess and Tahnee filled two saddlebags in the bedroom, Billy and Jason carried filled bags out the back door and strapped them on the packhorse. Bess and Tahnee came out, and Jason and Billy attached the saddlebags.

Bess handed Jason his jacket. "I've stitched the coins inside, just like before, all that we didn't squander buying your stuff." She smiled. Jason took the jacket, pulled it on.

"Thanks for this," Jason said, "and for everything you have done for us, this time and all the other times. We wouldn't have been able to manage without your help. If there's such a thing as angels, you're a pair."

Billy shook his head, looked aside. Bess ducked her head and wiped her eyes with a hand.

The four friends stood silently, waiting. "You're off then," said Billy. "I won't ask where you're going."

"And I won't tell you," said Jason. "Wouldn't want you to have to lie if you're ever questioned. Even though you lie pretty good." Jason smiled.

Bess reached for Tahnee, and they embraced, holding each other. They separated, Bess looking only at Tahnee. "You and me, Tahnee, we know who the real Californians are. You and me. We know we belong to the country. All these other people are just passing through." She looked in Tahnee's eyes, unsmiling. Tahnee embraced her again, pulled back and kissed her cheek.

Bess reached for Jason and hugged him. "You and this good woman, take care of yourselves. Listen to Tahnee. You have more to learn from her than she does from you." She said this without smiling. She patted his cheek.

Billy extended a hand to Jason, and he took it. "Jason, I wish you and Tahnee the best. You're two good people."

Jason and Tahnee untied their reins and mounted. Billy handed the reins of the packhorse to Jason. They turned their mounts and rode slowly from the yard. They waved to Bess and Billy, standing on the back porch, shadows in the darkness.

They rode in the meadow behind the row of shops and houses. Leaving the last house behind, they fell into the main track, clearly visible in the bright moonlight that led through open country westward toward Stockton.

After an hour, they turned north, breaking a new trail through the tall grasses. They looked eastward toward the dark mountain range where a faint glow showed at the crest. A new day was coming.

*****

# Afterword and Acknowledgements

If I were to list all of the people who assisted in the writing of this narrative, the dozens who offered snippets of information, suggestions, musings, advice, criticism and glasses of wine, the list would be very long. So I simply thank them and hope they find that I have distilled their data satisfactorily.

I am particularly grateful to the Pacific Critique Alliance for their careful reading of the narrative and for their comments, corrections and inspiration, namely Betsy Keithcart, Jennifer Hoffman, Rana Banankhah, Pamela Pan, Lorraine Ramsey, Leslie Liberty, Mary Ellen Dempsey, Jan Alexander, Vickie Fitz, Jennifer Grainger, Mariah Parke, Alysse Adularia, Erin Okamoto, Dwight Richards and Daniel Hobbs. I could ask for no better editorial support. Saeid Ranankhah read and commented on the proof copy.

My thanks to John Horst for putting the right guns in the hands of my characters.

Contrary to popular belief, novelists do not make it all up. At least, those who write historical fiction must place their story in the context of what actually happened. Novels customarily do not include a bibliography, but a partial list of books consulted might be useful to the reader who wishes to investigate the historical context of the story. Among the sources consulted for this novel, these were the most useful:

Bancroft, Hubert Howe, *History of California*, Vol. VI, 1848-1859

Barrett, Samuel A., and Edward W. Gifford, *Indian Life of Yosemite Region: Miwok Material Culture*

Bates, Craig D., *The Miwok in Yosemite: Southern Miwok Life, History, and Language in the Yosemite Region.*

Bunnell, Lafayette Houghton, *Discovery of the Yosemite & the Indian War of 1851*

Caughey, John Walton, *The California Gold Rush*

Clarke, Galen, *Indians of the Yosemite Valley and Vicinity*

Colton, Rev. Walter, *Three Years in California*

Heizer, Robert F., and Albert B. Elsasser, *The Natural World of the California Indians*

La Pena, Frank, Craig D. Bates, and Steven P. Medley, compilers, *Legends of the Yosemite Miwok*

Margolin, Malcolm, ed., *The Way We Lived: California Indian Stories, Songs & Reminiscences*

Merriam, C. Hart, ed., *The Dawn of the World: Myths and Tales of the Miwok Indians of California*

Muir, John, *The Yosemite*

Parker, Julia F., *It Will Live Forever: Traditional Yosemite Indian Acorn Preparation*

Russell, Carl Parcher, *One Hundred Years in Yosemite*

Wilson, Herbert Carl, *The Lore and the Lure of the Yosemite: The Indians; Their Customs, Legends, and Beliefs, and the Story of Yosemite*

# About the Author

Harlan Hague, Ph.D., is a native Texan who has lived in Japan and England. His travels have taken him to about eighty countries and dependencies and a circumnavigation of the globe.

Hague is a prize-winning historian and award-winning novelist. History specialties are exploration and trails, California's Mexican era, American Indians and the environment. His novels range from Japan to the American West, all with romance themes and, in one, a bit of science fiction. In addition to history, biography and fiction, he has written travel articles and a bit of fantasy. His screenplays are making the rounds.

For more about what he has done and what he is doing, see his website at harlanhague.us. Hague lives in California.

Made in the USA
San Bernardino, CA
27 November 2018